PRAISE FOR JANE FUTCHER'S HEAT

"Jane Futcher is a fiendishly good writer. Her latest collection, *Heat: Stories of Love and Desire*, places Futcher squarely among that luminous trinity: Jeanette Winterson, Sarah Waters, and Emma Donoghue. Futcher has a wicked sense of humor. During the brief spells that her main character isn't entangled, *a deux*, in a pair of silk sheets, she is thrashing about in an existential fog. Why, after all, limit a lesbian to ecstasy?

"Come to think of it, forget Jeanette, Sarah, and Emma. Futcher's subversive juxtaposition of clit nibbles and funny bone tickles puts her in a league all her own."

MARNY HALL, PH.D., AUTHOR OF *THE LAVENDER COUCH* AND *THE LESBIAN LOVE COMPANION: HOW TO SURVIVE EVERYTHING FROM HEARTTHROB TO HEARTBREAK*

"Author Jane Futcher crushes the tired old male myth that women can't have sex without a penis. Given today's political climate, it seems everyone has to have a penis to exist. However, in *Heat*, Ms. Futcher gives us such great news: Sex is for women and best with other women! Whether seducing Mom's best friend on a Caribbean beach, getting laid by a sexy femme with an enormous strap-on, or enchanting a petite ballroom dancer (while her mother is dying a few blocks away), Futcher explores lesbian passion, fantasy, fun and frailty from childhood to cremation. Try it — I mean, REALLY TRY IT! You'll like it. As Chappell Roan would say, 'It's a femininomenon!'"

JOANN LOULAN, AUTHOR OF *LESBIAN SEX; LESBIAN PASSION; LESBIAN EROTIC DANCE*

"Every lesbian will want to read a book about a woman's sexual yearnings, encounters and long-term relationships. In *Heat,* the erotic stories of popular author Jane Futcher take you inside a second-grader's fantasy marriage to her beguiling schoolteacher; a woman's first lesbian encounter with her boyfriend's sister; a lesbian embracing her inner tomboy; a woman's rage at her wife's ex-lovers, and the romantic temptations posed by life with a partner who is often away. Readers will enjoy the humor, love, erotic passion, and emotional roadblocks in these stories."

ESTHER ROTHBLUM, PH.D., PROFESSOR EMERITA AND
EDITOR OF THE JOURNAL OF LESBIAN STUDIES

"These stories of lesbian love and fantasy will keep readers as captivated as a Shonda Rhimes TV series."

NANETTE GARTRELL, M.D., PSYCHIATRIST AND AUTHOR OF
MY ANSWER IS NO

"Jane Futcher's *Heat* captures the experience of coming out and exploring the excitement and intrigue of becoming a lesbian. The book is a wild ride through loss and joy as the character of Jill survives and thrives both steamy adventures and compromising situations. When she finds a partner who understands her and a community that knows her well, she heals her past and enjoys a present filled with wisdom and deep trust."

THE REV. JANE A. SPAHR, LESBIAN ACTIVIST AND CO-
FOUNDER OF THAT ALL MAY FREELY SERVE

Praise for Futcher's Novels

"*Dream Lover* is absolutely wonderful — compelling, humane, sometimes funny, sometimes sad, beautifully written and wise."

ANNE LAMOTT, AUTHOR OF BIRD BY BIRD AND OPERATING INSTRUCTIONS

"Jane Futcher's *Crush* presents the confusing, terrifying dilemmas that accompany any step out of the narrow band of acceptable behavior that society tolerates."

DOROTHY ALLISON, AUTHOR OF BASTARD OUT OF CAROLINA

"Few young-adult writers have succeeded in capturing the dialogue and internal voice of confused young men with the authenticity and power of *Promise Not to Tell*, by Jane Futcher."

PATRICIA HOLT, SAN FRANCISCO CHRONICLE

OTHER BOOKS BY JANE FUTCHER

Crush

Marin: The Place, The People

Promise Not to Tell

Dream Lover

Women Gone Wild

HEAT

STORIES OF LOVE AND DESIRE

JANE FUTCHER

Tehom Center Publishing is a 501(c)3 nonprofit publishing feminist and queer authors, with a commitment to elevate BIPOC writers. Its face and voice is Rev. Dr. Angela Yarber.

Paperback ISBN: 978-1-966655-22-0

Ebook ISBN: 978-1-966655-24-4

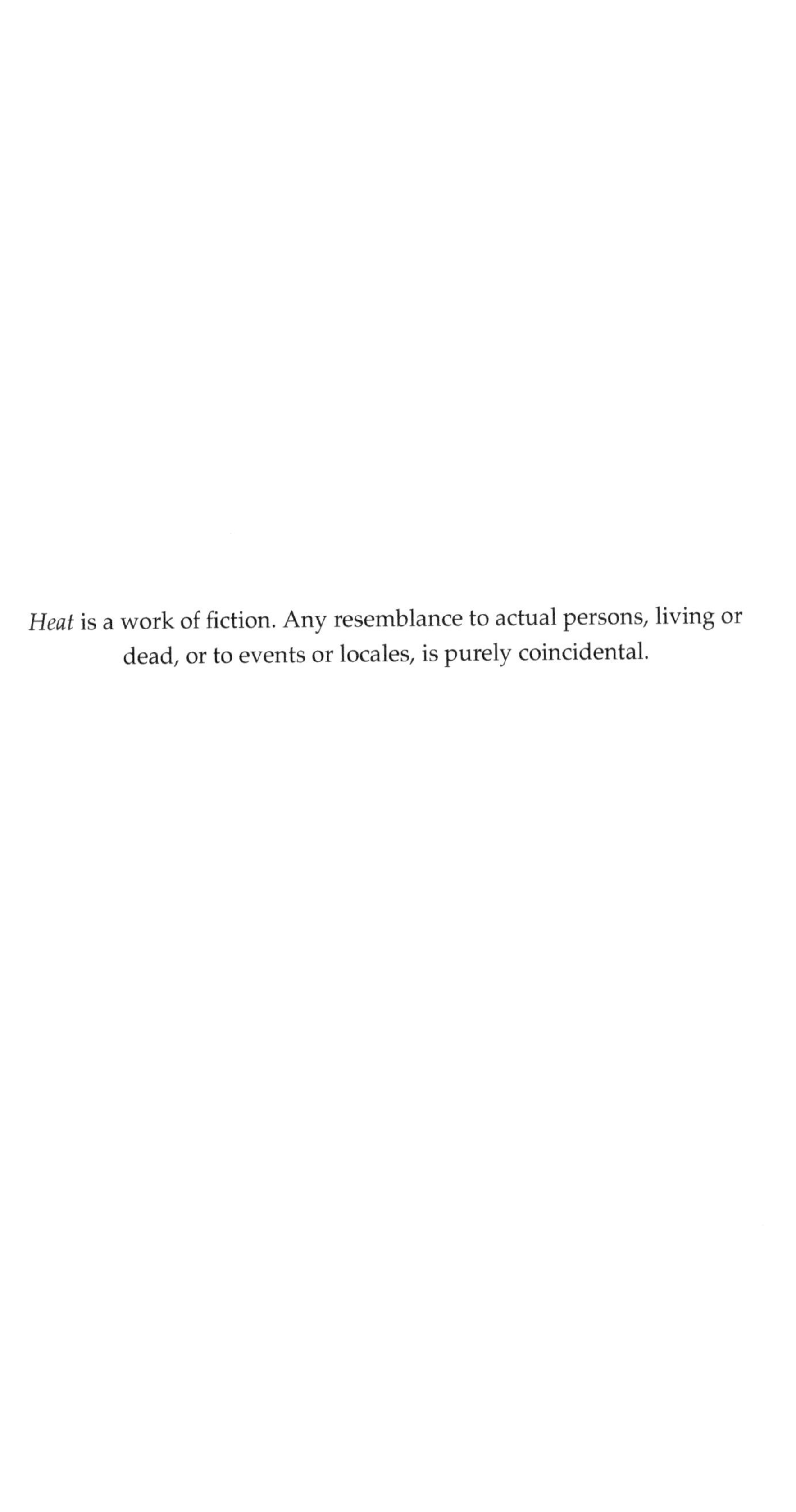

Heat is a work of fiction. Any resemblance to actual persons, living or dead, or to events or locales, is purely coincidental.

For Erin

WHERE THESE STORIES WERE FIRST PUBLISHED

Betty Loves Veronica
First published as "Betty and Veronica" in *Uniform Sex: Erotic Stories of Women in Service*, Linnea Due, Editor, Alyson Publications, Inc., 2000

Wednesday Afternoons
First published in *Lesbian Adventure Stories*, Mara Wild and Mikaya Heart, Editors, Tough Dove Books, 1994

Bagels and Mink
First published as "Pale Blue Hydrangea" in *Afterglow*, Karen Barber, Editor, Alyson Publications, Inc., 1993

Caribbean Wave
First published in *Hot Ticket*, Linnea Due, Editor, Alyson Publications, Inc., 1997

Rough Crossing
First published in *Heatwave*, Lucy Jane Bledsoe, Editor, Alyson Publications, Inc., 1995

In Another Country

First published in *Harrington Lesbian Fiction Quarterly*, Judith P. Stelboum, Editor, *Vol. 1, Number 2*, 2000

Past Lives

First published in *Bushfire: Stories of Lesbian Desire*, Karen Barber, Editor, Alyson Publications, Inc., 1991

Ex-Lovers' Weekend

First published as "Leaving Liza" in *Journal of Lesbian Studies*, Vol. 8, Nos. 3 & 4, *Lesbian Ex-Lover Relationships: Under-Estimated, Under-Theorized, Under-Valued?* Jacqueline E. Weinstock and Esther D. Rothblum, Editors, Harrington Park Press, an imprint of Haworth Press, Inc., Binghamton, NY 13904-1580, 2004

Wild Iris

First published in *Bedroom Eyes*, Leslea Newman, Editor, Alyson Publications, Inc., 2002

A WORD FROM JANE FUTCHER

Lust is a magical thing. It can lead to pleasure and love, heartache and disaster — often all four.

For most of history, lesbian love, lust, attraction and ecstasy were hidden from view. But in the 1990s, several LGBTQ publishers, particularly Alyson Publications, Inc., in Boston, began printing anthologies by and about lesbians, with one caveat to contributors: The stories must be erotic.

As the author of an early lesbian coming-of-age novel called *Crush*, I happily submitted stories to Alyson's *Bushfire, Afterglow, Hot Ticket* and *Uniform Sex*, among them. I didn't have to search far to find material: Lesbian passions, crushes, attractions and obsessions, often invisible to mainstream America, were a driving force in my own life as well as the lives of most of the lesbians I knew.

With the demise of many LGBTQ publishers and bookstores in the early 2000s, the outlets for lesbian erotic tales and short stories disappeared. But our longings, crushes, affairs, betrayals, couplings, marriages, and wild hook-ups remain today as present as they ever were. I hope that *Heat: Stories of Love and Desire* honors our lust and our love, our heartaches and successful marriages, our failed affairs and creative adaptations. Above all, I hope this book entertains you, as it has me, with its lust and longing, fantasy and fun, ménages and mistakes.

Jane Futcher
Santa Rosa, CA
2025

CONTENTS

BETTY LOVES VERONICA

My sister and I were both in love with Emma. Her easy mastery of any sport she tried, her wise brown eyes, her freckles and ready smile, the cool distance she kept from the other summer kids held us in a state of longing each August, when our parents rented one of her father's cottages on the Maine coast.

Emma went to boarding school, but her family lived in the village year-round, in a rambling white clapboard farmhouse on the high ground above the beach, with a gnarled apple tree in the side yard and a red garage that had once been the carriage house and hay barn. Some of the summer kids said Emma was stuck-up and spoiled because she was an only child, and her father gave her an entire section of the bath-houses he owned for all her rafts and snorkels, fishing gear, skimmers and inner tubes.

"She's not a snob," we'd say, thrilled that for some unknown reason Emma hung out with my sister and me and not the summer kids her own age from Philadelphia's Main Line and swanky suburbs in St. Louis and Cincinnati. "You're jealous because she won't let you read her comics," we'd tell the Emma-skeptics.

I think I'd wanted to touch Emma since I was ten, when I first inhaled Noxzema on her shoulders as she and my sister and I lay on

Emma's bed eating the amazing white cake with blue icing she'd dyed with food coloring and reading her comics. Emma had what we thought must be the world's largest collection of comic books, an entire walk-in closet stacked with crisp, clean copies of *Little Lulu*, *Superman*, *Donald Duck* and *Mickey Mouse*. As we got older, our affection for talking animals gave way to an interest in *Betty and Veronica* and *True Romance* comics. I always imagined I was one of those square-jawed young men in a plaid sports jacket vying for the love and admiration of the gorgeous, narrow-waisted girls who cried crystal tears if a handsome boy rejected them.

The first evening that we arrived each summer, Emma would come over with her father to Kittiwake or Gray Gull or Pine Cottage and stand in the doorway, hands tucked in the pockets of her faded jeans, hair in pigtails, boyish but somehow glamorously feminine in her striped T-shirt. Our fathers, friends since boyhood, would plan their annual adventure in the sailing dory to some far island while my sister and I, bashful and shy, would get to know Emma all over again.

"Emma," we'd say, for she was two years older than me and a year older than my older sister, "Want to row the dinghy over to Rock Island tomorrow? Or walk to the tidepools on Heart Point?"

"Sure," she'd say. "And I have something for you." She'd run to the car and bring us a stack of fresh comics, always loaning them on one condition — that we return them to her without any smudges, rips or fingerprints. It was an awesome responsibility because we were naturally messy children, but we always promised to try.

We never got enough of Emma, who was always hurrying off after our morning swims in the ocean for tennis or golf or diving lessons at the Abenaki Club. We could only snag her later in the day on those rare afternoons when her mother hadn't signed her up for any improvement classes. She'd invite us to her big white house on the hill to lounge on her bed reading comics.

The summer of '62, when I was fifteen, and my sister was sixteen and Emma was seventeen, Emma's father came down to our cottage to see us on our first night in Maine. His eyes were red from reading legal briefs and spread sheets, and his shoulders were more stooped than we'd ever seen them.

"Where's Emma?" we asked, disappointed.

"She's got a job this summer." His Boston accent was quirky and kind of exotic.

"Not here?" My sister glared at my mother, as if Emma's absence were somehow Mother's fault.

"She's cleaning rooms at the Wentworth Hotel in Portsmouth. Lives in the employee dorm. Said she wanted to be financially independent. She makes a dollar fifty an hour. I offered to send her to Europe with some of the other girls in her class, or to triple her salary if she'd help us clean our rentals, but she wouldn't hear of it."

"Jeez," I said. The thought of a vacation without Emma was bleak.

"Fuck," swore my sister, who had started using bad language.

"Meg, please," my mother said. The troubles between them, which lasted a lifetime, were getting very bad.

On our third day at Gray Gull, the telephone rang.

My mother answered and handed me the phone. "For you, Jill."

It was Emma, inviting me to visit her at the Wentworth. "I have Thursday afternoon off. We can do something fun like rent a pedal boat on the lake. Don't tell anyone, OK?" Since my mother and father and sister were all listening, not telling anyone was hard to do.

"I'll try," I said. How would I get there without a car?

She gave me the number of the pay phone in the dorm. "Call me when you know what time you're coming."

"Bye," I said, staring down at the police emergency number taped to the bottom of the telephone.

"Who was it?" my sister asked.

"Emma," I whispered.

"Emma? For you?" My sister's eyes narrowed.

"She wants me to come visit on Thursday."

My sister closed Jean Paul Sartre's *Nausea*. "What about me?"

"She didn't mention you," I managed. I wanted Emma to myself. I didn't want Meg to come along. On Thursday, when my father, after some secret prodding from me, announced he was driving to Portsmouth to buy a new anchor for the dory, I feigned indifference. I knew if I said I wanted to go, my sister would want to come, too. As Dad was pulling out of the driveway, I jumped in the car.

"Can you drop me at the Wentworth Hotel?" I said, as we turned onto Route 1A.

He glanced at me oddly. "Is this something to do with Emma?"

"Emma has the afternoon off." I forced the emotion from my voice, "We're going to..." I paused. What were we going to do? "Rent a pedal boat or something."

"Your sister didn't want to come?"

"I'm not sure," I lied. "I think we're taking a break." People were always taking a break from things. Why shouldn't my sister and I take one? Just one hitch. I'd never called Emma to tell her I was coming. What if she wasn't there?

On the top floor, down a long hall in a three-story, yellow wood-frame dorm building, I found Emma lying on one of the twin beds in a tiny, bare room at the Wentworth-by-the-Sea in her yellow uniform. I almost threw up my nerves were so bad. The cotton dress came just to her knees; a white apron was tied around her hips, and her hair was twisted up in a sort of a bun.

"Hey," she smiled, pushing a long strand of hair from her eyes. "You made it. How long do we have?"

I swallowed. "Daddy's buying an anchor."

"How long does that take?" She stood up. "This uniform is embarrassing."

"It looks nice. You look..." Good, I wanted to say but was that too forward. She actually looked like a movie-star to me, like my favorite actress, Shirley MacLaine. Her breasts seemed to heave beneath the yellow and white stripes. She was someone from my dreams. Emma had changed. She wasn't a kid in blue jeans anymore. She'd grown up.

We walked along the water, the huge white wooden hotel looming behind us, the ocean in front of us. It seemed weird and kind of sad that an amazing athlete and brilliant student like Emma was cleaning hotel rooms when she could have been out playing tennis or golf or or traveling through Europe with her boarding school friends. "Why are you working here?" I asked.

"To get away from the parents," she said, staring out at the sea.

"You'd rather be here than in Europe?"

She lit a cigarette, a Tareyton, and offered me one. I lit one and tried not to throw up. "I hate my parents," she was saying. "They think if I go to the club enough and get a golf handicap I'll become like them. That's the last thing I want." She smiled at me with such affection I nearly fainted. "I told Mom I want to be a lobsterman and not a debutante. She nearly shit."

I bit my lip. Emma and my sister were both swearing a lot these days. But Emma had so much... what? What everybody wanted — looks, brains, athletic skill, everything. And she was rich. And early acceptance at Radcliffe. Why wasn't she happy?

"Hey, Emma!" Above us, on the road, a guy in a white shirt and a black bow tie, his dark hair smoothed back in a kind of Elvis conch, was waving at her. She didn't wave back.

"Who's that?" I asked.

"Nobody," she said, walking faster. "Don't talk to him."

"I think your uniform is kind of cool," I said, changing the subject.

She curtsied to me. "Our specials today, Madam, are lobster thermidor, steak *au poivre*, and prime ribs with sautéed French beans and a baked potato."

"I thought you cleaned rooms."

"I got promoted. They're a bunch of idiots." She stamped out her cigarette.

"Have you ever dropped a plate on somebody's lap? You've got to be coordinated to be a waitress."

Emma chewed her lip, then suddenly, without warning, took my hand. "I've missed you so much. I'm sorry I didn't write you this year."

I swallowed. I had written her five or six times over the winter, but I stopped because she never answered back. Now, the softness of her skin made feathers in my stomach. "You're so busy."

"I saved your letters," she said, stopping by the sea wall, where some painted red and white lobster buoys were drying in the sun. The air smelled of seaweed and salt. "I read them over and over."

"You did?" My eyes were fixed on the white napkin poking out from a pocket just above her breast. We had come to a small cove.

Emma pulled a little comb from the back of her head, and her long brown hair tumbled down. I don't know how, but somehow I managed to reach out and touch a strand without my hands shaking.

"I'm fucked up, you know." Her brown eyes locked on mine, and her hand tightened around my fingers.

"Me too," I gulped, so close I could smell the almond of the Jergens lotion she'd rubbed on her skin.

"You're not fucked up," she said, squeezing my hand. "You're great. You make me laugh. You're original."

"Is original good?"

"It's all that matters to me." Her arm reached around my waist. "My mother is shitfaced every night. You know that, right?"

"What?" It was hard to think about Emma's mom with Emma so close.

"She's a lush. So is my father." Her arm tightened around me.

My fingers froze. "I've never seen your mother drunk."

She nodded. "Yep. Passes out every night on the couch in front of the TV. My father holds it better than she does."

"I always thought your mother was sleeping."

"Right." Emma smiled bitterly, pulling me down onto the sand next to her as if she were one of the dream girls in *True Romance* comics.

I glanced at her uniform. "Won't you get dirty?"

"Who gives a flying fuck? I hate this uniform."

"It makes you look—"

"Ridiculous," she said.

"Kind of sexy," I said.

She glanced behind us at the huge hotel and looked at her watch. "Let's go back to my room. My roommate won't be back until dinner."

"Your room?" I couldn't breathe.

"It would be fun, don't you think? To lie down?"

I was blushing. She seemed so decisive and experienced.

We walked back up the beach, around the guest parking lot filled with dozens of Cadillacs and Continentals, across the gravel path to the funky clapboard employee dorm, where tons of girls were now sitting on the steps, smoking and wearing little yellow-and-white uniforms like Emma's, with handkerchiefs in the pockets and their hair in buns.

"Hi, Emma." That same guy with his dark hair slicked back, in tight black pants and a white shirt with a black bow tie, tried to grab Emma's elbow.

"Leave me alone," she said, pulling her arm away. "I can't stand him," she whispered as we started up the steps. "What an idiot."

"Is he your boyfriend?"

She stopped on the staircase. "I don't have a boyfriend."

We hiked up two more flights of dark, musty steps, and into the long dark hallway, where Emma opened the door to her room with a key from her pocket. The two twin beds were separated by a sliver of bare floor and a tiny nightstand with an unshaded lamp.

She looked at me. "Let's undress."

"Undress?"

"You don't have to," she said. "Let's just hold each other."

We lay on top of the scratchy green wool military blanket, not touching at first. Emma's Jergens lotion smelled heavenly.

"I'm attracted to you, you know," she said.

"To me?" I swallowed as her lips inched closer to mine. And then somehow we were kissing, little soft kisses, like guppies in a tank or minnows that nibble your toes in a pond. Suddenly, just like in romance comics, a diamond tear glistened on Emma's cheek. "I've really missed you," she said. "I don't know why I took this stupid job. I wish I were home with you."

"Is it a guy?" I said, watching a small black spider drop down from the ceiling.

"A guy?" She looked puzzled.

"That's why you're here. Because of that waiter or something?" Her knee was between mine, and she was unzipping my red plaid shorts that were hand-me-downs from my sister.

"No way." She shook her head solemnly. "I couldn't stand another summer at home. Too depressing."

"But your dad said you could have gone to Europe." She was touching my white cotton underpants, and I was untying her apron. I kissed her with an open mouth and felt her pressing against my hips, her knee between my legs, and I was coming undone. Maybe this feeling was why I liked riding horses and riding our bannisters at home. We were moving all over each other, and all of a sudden, she moaned, so loud it kind of shocked me. It wasn't peaceful, like being out in her dinghy or floating on canvas rafts in the waves. Everything was spinning and wet and confusing.

"I really like you," she said. She was lying naked now, face up, beside me. "Did you come?"

"Come?" I swallowed, looking at her round, soft breasts.

"Get off?"

"I don't know." I wasn't sure what it was exactly. I looked at my watch and started to get dressed. "I'd like to do this again. I really like, you know, being with you."

"I like being with you," she said. "I'd like to know you better."

"I thought you loved my sister more than me," I said, zipping up my shorts.

"I love Meg, but not in the same way." She kicked her legs over the side of the bed and pulled her bra and uniform back on quickly. "She's more my friend."

"Are we friends?" I said.

"We're more than friends now," she laughed, mussing my hair with her fingers.

"I'm sorry your folks are alcoholics."

Her eyes grew suddenly dark. "Mom's so messed up. Scary so. She's going to kill someone in a head-on one of these days." She shook her head, turning as she opened the door, her face lightening. "I never did that before."

"I thought..."

"Not with a girl." She touched my arm.

I looked at my watch again. "Dad's probably down there waiting."

"What if I took the whole day off tomorrow? Can you come back?"

I blinked. "Meg would want to come. She can drive now. She could bring me, maybe."

She thought for a minute. "I'll come home next Thursday, and you can spend the night. Just you and me. I won't be wearing this fucking uniform."

"I really like it," I gulped.

She looked eager and ready. "I've got a couple *Little Lulus* you haven't seen."

"Wow. I love *Lulu*."

"I know." As she laughed, a bell shrieked through the dorm. "Oh, fuck," she said. "Dinner's early tonight." She straightened her uniform. "Am I wrinkled?"

"A little." I tried to fix her collar. And the little napkin in her pocket was all askew.

"Fuck it." She twisted her hair back into a bun. "Fuck all of them."

"Your customers might think you've been sleeping on the beach."

"Good." She winked at me. She was so much more advanced than I was.

We held hands walking down the stairs. "Say hello to your father for me," she said as we reached the parking lot. "I'll call you about the weekend, OK?"

"OK." I kept my eyes on the curve of her waist, trying to imprint her image onto my retinas. She grabbed me and kissed me, right there in front of my father and the waiters and bus boys and waitresses as they hurried to their shifts. One of guys whistled at us. I blushed getting in the car. Emma shrugged, waved to me and disappeared into the hotel service entrance.

She never called. She wrote me at home six months later from a town called Kitzbuhel in Austria. "I'm studying German. I hate German, but I got pregnant and had an abortion in Boston. Mom arranged it. Stupid me. I miss you."

My sister didn't come to Maine the following summer. She got a job selling handbags in the garment district in New York before her college started.

Emma's mother came over to Kittiwake Cottage one night just after we got there in August. I could see how she was kind of drunk, and I think she was crying. She told my mom that Emma had refused to come back to the U.S.A. even though Radcliffe had deferred her enrollment a year. And she'd ordered her mother to throw out her comic book collection, every last one.

"Oh, no," I gulped.

"All but the *Little Lulus,*" she said. "She asked me to save them for you, Emma. And I did."

The next day, when I came to retrieve the *Little Lulus,* I lingered as long as I could in Emma's empty comic-book closet. I could still smell the pulp of the pages, feel the touch of Emma's fingers, see her lean, lovely body in that yellow uniform in her small, sad room at the Wentworth Hotel.

My folks didn't go to Maine after that. My sister dropped out of college and wouldn't speak to them and I started college, and, Emma was somewhere in Europe going to the Sorbonne, I think. The whole idea of a family vacation kind of fizzled out because we weren't a family anymore, just individuals wondering what happened. I still think about Emma. I have a dream that maybe one day she'll come home, and we'll pick up where we left off. Wouldn't that be something?

WEDNESDAY AFTERNOONS

Not every eight-year-old girl can transform herself into a handsome, sexy, *True Romance* comic book hero, but I could, and did, in 1955, during my second-grade year at the Canterbury School in Baltimore, Maryland. Canterbury is an expensive little school, which, years later, I was informed by a classmate at our fifteenth reunion, used its well-heeled students as guinea pigs to develop mail-order home instruction for the children of missionaries, yachtsmen, and CIA agents living in remote regions of the world. At the time I didn't know that I was a pawn of the U.S. espionage establishment. I was just a pale little girl with Dutch-bobbed hair who dreamed of marrying her second-grade teacher.

I know what you are thinking. An eight-year-old cannot have an affair with a twenty-five-year-old woman. But in my dreams I did exactly that. Miss Cherry and I were mad for each other — wild, willing, consenting adults.

She was not like Canterbury's other female teachers, who were strict, stiff, and elderly. She was a siren, the school's Marilyn Monroe, with her platinum pageboy, wide red lips, and pinup body. An elegant string of pearls caressed the creamy curve of her neck above her cashmere sweaters and inviting cleavage. Her voice was low and soothing as she called out, and we repeated, the "puhs and tuhs and thuhs" in phonics drills, causing chills to rise up my spine.

Greta Van Slyck, my best friend, was also in love with Miss Cherry. By mid-October, in Miss Cherry's presence, Greta and I had become one person, one single, dreamy, good-looking suitor who planned to rescue Miss Cherry on a dazzling white stallion, like the Lone Ranger, taking her away from the drab halls of Canterbury and the red-faced leers of Mr. Draberfus, the boys' playground supervisor and football coach.

On Wednesday afternoons, the school released us at 1 p.m. instead of the usual 4:30. On this particular Wednesday, Greta and I lingered near our lockers by the classroom door hoping to give Miss Cherry the note that we had composed together at Greta's house, informing her of our love and asking for her hand in marriage.

We were breathless when Miss Cherry appeared at the classroom door, our spelling tests in hand, her red lips parted in a surprised smile. "Hello, girls."

"Hi, Miss Cherry," we answered in unison, gripping our book bags.

"Give her the note," I whispered to Greta. But Greta panicked, shoved our proposal in her pocket and ran down the polished hallway.

"Greta!" I called.

But she was gone, down into the lobby and outside to the turn-around, where everyone's mother waited in their cars to pick up their kids.

"I can't ask her to marry me, Jill," she whispered, when I caught up with her. "It's a sin."

"What?" I was afraid I'd cry. "You said you wanted to marry her."

"I do, Jill. I did. But I'd have to go to confession." Greta's eyes widened as she looked over my shoulder. "Our priest is Mummy's second-cousin once removed."

Suddenly, there was Miss Cherry, a red handbag the color of her lips and fingernails, dangling from her arm. "Can I give you girls a lift somewhere?"

At age eight, home was the only place we were ever allowed to go after school. "No, thank you," Greta said, grabbing my arm. "Mummy's waiting for us. We've got dancing class today." I looked up. Sure enough, Mrs. Van Slyck's gray Dodge was double-parked by the portico. I turned, defeated, following Greta to her mother's car, but my heart remained steadfastly with Miss Cherry, reviewing what I *wished* I'd said — and done — in a world I feared might never be mine.

"I'd love a ride, Miss Cherry." I gripped my bookbag, hoping she didn't see my knees shaking. I hated dancing class, was no good at the box step and the foxtrot with a boy's sweaty hands dragging on my sash.

"My car's just down the street, Jill," Miss Cherry said, taking my hand and leaning so close I could smell her Lilies of the Valley perfume. I could see Greta staring at us in disbelief. Miss Cherry inserted the key into her two-toned, blue and cream Oldsmobile Super Rocket.

And that's when it happened. Suddenly, I was Jim, a handsome playboy wearing a navy blazer, Brooks Brothers shirt, striped tie, tan chinos and polished Weejuns. I glanced at myself in the rear-view mirror, thrilled to see that I looked like a cross between my two favorite movie stars — Roy Rogers and Pat Boone. Fingers grazing my palm, Miss Cherry handed me the keys, her brown eyes enveloping me in a gauzy haze. "Would you mind driving, Jim?"

Jim? I nearly corrected her, reminding her my name was Jill, but felt such a warm tingling in my legs I stopped myself. "Certainly, Miss Cherry," I said, circling the car, opening the driver's door and turning on the ignition as I had seen my parents do so often. I hoped the woman of my dreams did not realize that I'd never driven a car before. Lucky for me, her Olds Super Rocket was an automatic and far easier to steer than my parents' Chevy clutch and even the fat-tired Schwinn I pedaled around the neighborhood.

"Where to, Miss Cherry?" I said, in Jim Remington's cheerful baritone. The car was rolling smoothly past the school and down Wickford Road.

"No need to be so formal, Jim. Call me Eugenie." The tips of her red fingernails rested lightly on my knee. I managed the turn onto Overhill, and then, near Keswick, felt such a surge of happiness that I extended my right arm around Miss Cherry's shoulders as I'd seen Pat Boone do in *April Love*.

"Alone at last," whispered Miss Cherry. Her words turned my stomach to pink cotton candy while the rest of me lifted like a balloon. She kicked off her heels and curled her legs up under her.

"Gosh," I said. We were passing my parents' house on Roland Avenue. My mother was standing in the front yard pruning the thorny hedge by the sidewalk. I started to duck, but realized I didn't need to. I was Jim Remington; Mom wouldn't recognize me or see Miss Cherry inching those lovely painted fingers up my leg.

"I'd like to... spend some time alone with you, Jim," Miss Cherry said hoarsely.

"Good idea," I gulped. But where? The roof of the garages in the alley behind my house was one of my favorite hiding places, but I couldn't see Miss Cherry climbing up the rusty, sagging drainpipe in her skirt, stockings and high heels. Besides, the Rouse boys might see her from their tree fort in the sumac tree. And the soda fountain at Wagoner and Wagoner's Drugstore, my other favorite place, where I bought wax lips and Jujubes and red vines after school, would be swarming with kids now.

"How about the country club?" It was my playboy voice. "We can have..." I hesitated. "A drink." That's what my parents always wanted when they went to a country club. And why not? There was a bar downstairs hidden from the ballroom upstairs, where I was supposed to be dancing soon in my scratchy purple velvet dress, white socks and patent leather shoes.

Miss Cherry's eyes smoked and her titties, barely concealed by her cashmere sweater, rubbed against my chest. "Pull over now, Jimmy," she begged. "I can't wait."

I swerved into the parking lot of Resurrection Episcopal Church, where I went every Sunday with my parents. I prayed that Reverend Smiley was visiting the sick today, and that Mrs. Sadler, my Sunday

School teacher, was at home making wibbly-wobbly Jell-0 as she prepared next week's class on sin and absolution.

"I've looked forward to this moment for a long time," Miss Cherry whispered, her fingers undoing my necktie, her hot breath on my ear. She was a dream date, eager and encouraging, not prudish and prim like the girls in *True Romance* comics who always pulled away and slapped their dates at the first hint of monkey-business. I hoped she didn't see my goosebumps or feel my right leg twitch where her hand was touching me. I wished for one quick moment that Greta were here with us, could feel Miss Cherry's breasts pressing against me and smell her Lilies of the Valley perfume. This is what Greta and I had dreamed since we'd walked into her classroom in September. Greta would never believe that I was slipping my hand beneath Miss Cherry's sweater, and she didn't pull away. Far from it. "Undo my bra," she whispered, leaning slightly forward and helping me unfasten the clasp. It wasn't all that easy, but we managed it together.

"Oh, gosh." I could feel her bosoms in my hand. When our lips met, we both took off for the stars.

"You're so nice, Jimmy. So sexy."

"Because I love you, Miss Cherry," I said. "I'm in love with you."

"I'm in love with you, Jimmy." Miss Cherry's voice suggested movies and sunsets and carousels. "Will you bite my nipples?"

"Bite them?" I said, alarmed. The boys in teen comics never bit girls' bosoms.

"Please, Jimmy." She lay back on the seat and placed my hands on her cleavage. The sight of her womanly features waiting to receive me made me hiccup. She pulled my mouth to them. "My sweet captain," she gasped.

Oh, those words. I'd always wanted to be a captain or a lieutenant or even just a lowly corporal ever since Elvis had joined the Army. Trembling, I closed my lips around her nipples. She sighed in the key of angels. She was clinging to me, sliding beneath me, pulling me closer. Christmas trees blinked in my legs and Frank Sinatra sang "Bewitched" in my ears. Her knee between my legs caused celestial vibrations inside me. "Marry me, Miss Cherry," I cried. She had unbuttoned my shirt, was tracing circles on my undershirt with the tips of her fingers.

"You bet I'll marry you, Jimmy!"

I had dreamed of marrying Miss Cherry, and now it was going to happen. Her eyes opened wide, and for a moment I thought she was going to throw up. But no, she gasped and seemed very happy, hugging me and laughing, almost screeching. "Oh, Jimmy," she yelled. "You sure know what you're doing!"

"Thank you, Eugenie," I glowed. Knowing how jealous Greta would be helped me calm down after the scare of Miss Cherry's screaming. Was this what Reverend Smiley meant by "the fullness of joy" in his sermon last week?

Suddenly, a fist rapped the window. Electric with love, Miss Cherry and I quickly rearranged ourselves and rolled down the window. It was Reverend Smiley himself, his mild, Christian eyes studying Miss Cherry's bosom. Fortunately, he did not seem to recognize me although I was in his daughter Patricia's Sunday School class.

"Y'all being good?" he winked.

"Yes, sir, Reverend. We're engaged to be married," Miss Cherry said.

"Congratulations! God bless you."

"We were just going over to the club to have a drink," I said, turning on the ignition.

"To celebrate our..." Miss Cherry smiled beatifically. "Engagement."

"Y'all run along then. And be sure to use... protection. I'd be happy to officiate. When you're ready."

"Thank you, Reverend," Miss Cherry said, sweetly adjusting my tie.

"What's protection?" I asked.

We drove slowly up the club driveway, right between the fifteenth green and the sixteenth tee, and wouldn't you know, my dancing-class carpool was just ahead of us. Greta turned and stared, shocked by the sight of me driving Miss Cherry's Rocket Olds with our teacher cuddled in my arm. Miss Cherry and I played it safe, waiting near the white clapboard clubhouse until all the children's carpools had unloaded.

"Name your poison," I said, imitating my father as I guided Miss Cherry into the cool, dark bar, my hand resting lightly on her waist. Greta would never look for us here; children weren't allowed in the saloon.

"I'll drink anything. As long as it's with you, Jim," she whispered, her breath hot in my ear.

As we sank into the soft leather booth, I heard the saxophone, slap bass, and piano upstairs playing a foxtrot for the little children. How glad I was to be a man, to be cool, suave Jim Remington gazing into Miss Cherry's endless brown eyes, and not Jill Remington, forcing a smile upstairs as I tried to follow a boy's lead, his sweaty palms dragging my sash.

"Afternoon, Mr. Remington, Miss Cherry," said Henry, the bartender, bowing slightly. "What'll it be?"

Miss Cherry leaned back dreamily. "We'll have two dry martinis, Henry."

I scribbled my name on the tab when Henry returned, raised my glass and gazed into Miss Cherry's dilated pupils. "To us," I said, repeating the words I'd heard my parents say at cocktail time. I drew the glass to my lips and swallowed. "Whoa!" I coughed. I felt like I'd slugged a pint of gasoline.

"What's wrong?" Miss Cherry took my hand. "You alright, Jimmy?"

"Oh, sure." I stifled a gag, afraid I'd vomit, then wiped my mouth with a napkin. But already I was beginning to relax. No wonder my parents liked cocktail time so much. One sip of that martini and I forgot to feel shy. "We'll do this soon again, Eugenie," I said, using her Christian name again. "How 'bout every Wednesday?"

"I'd adore that," she answered, her hand finding mine beneath the table. Outside, the flag on the eighteenth green seemed to welcome me to the adult world of pleasure, power, romance and love.

"Jill!" my mother shouted from the kitchen. "Hurry up! You'll be late to school."

I was a nervous wreck. I couldn't decide what to wear, pulling everything out of my closet and finally settling on my blue plaid smock dress, white socks and leather oxfords. By that time, I was so late, I couldn't walk to school; Mom had to drive me. My heart pounded as I curtsied to the principal, who scowled at me for being late, and tiptoed down the silent halls of Canterbury, hanging my jacket in my wooden locker and entering the classroom. Twenty-five faces stared up at me.

"Good morning, Jilly," Miss Cherry said with a smile, writing something in her attendance book and handing me my spelling test. There were red marks all over the paper. "May I see you at recess, dear," Miss Cherry announced in a neutral voice. Had she forgotten everything? I kind of hoped so.

"You're in trouble," Greta whispered.

When the bell rang for recess, I waited by Miss Cherry's desk, face ashen, knees wobbling while Nan Whitby packed up the silly robin's nest she'd brought for show and tell. When she was gone, Miss Cherry did something I had never seen her do at recess — she closed the classroom door. My heart pounded like a gong I was sure she could hear.

"Jill," she said. "Your past four spelling tests have been very disappointing. And I know you're a bright girl. Are you OK? Is something upsetting you? You seem a little distracted in class. Everything alright at home?"

"I'm not very good at spelling." I could hardly talk. "Never have been."

She nodded in a kindly way. "Was there something you and Greta wanted to tell me yesterday when you were waiting for me?"

"Oh, no," I said, my hands beginning to sweat. Had she read my thoughts? Seen my dreams? "We just. You know. We really like you." I was blushing so hard my head was about to explode.

"You're sweet," she said, closing her grade book. "And I like you, too. I'm glad all's well at home. I won't keep you. I know you love kickball."

"I do, I do!" I cried, pulling on my jacket. I couldn't get out of there fast enough. I didn't want Miss Cherry to take off her bra or kiss my ear. I wanted to get outside and kick the ball so hard and high it soared over the girls' fence and into the boys' playground, smacking Mr. Draberfus on the head as my classmates hooted and clapped with joy and admiration.

But late at night, Miss Cherry returned, in technicolor. Wednesdays will always be sacred to me.

BAGELS AND MINK

It is a Saturday afternoon in mid-November, and the air is cold but not bitter. I am standing on a tree-lined street in suburban Rye, New York, in front of a neo-Tudor house, about to meet Rick's sister and brother-in-law for the first time. It is 1972 — before AIDS, before Rick met Danny, before I had slept with a woman and had given up my quest to be straight. Rick has told his sister that our relationship is serious, and he's eager to introduce me to his family.

On the drive from Philadelphia, Rick entertains me with tales of gay life in Philadelphia — the bars where he hangs out, the spot at Rittenhouse Square where Main Line stockbrokers cruise for boys, the marsh by the airport where the rough trade lurks. I am excited by the talk — my only contact with the gay world. I tell him about the producer at work who turns me on when she leans over my desk, her cleavage close to my shoulder, showing me the correct way to clean and glass-mount slides for the high-school assembly shows we're creating.

Rick and I are both nervous about spending the night with Victoria and Hal. We are starting to be a couple, but we have never slept together, and we are both gay — he actively, me in tortured silence, except with him. Under those circumstances, it's hard to feel too comfortable anywhere.

Now, here I am, in this well-heeled suburb of New York, near Long Island Sound, where the children play with Tuggy Tooters and Happy Hoppers, and their mothers pile take-out sushi and bags of gourmet groceries into their shiny European cars. Here now are Hal and Victoria coming down the flagstone walk of their large, faux Tudor, three-story house to greet us. Hal is much shorter than Rick, but dark and good-looking, wears starchy blue Levi's and a blue chambray shirt — the perfect leisure outfit for a successful Madison Avenue TV adman. Victoria is taller and lean, with a surprising suntan for November, straight brown hair, and huge, slightly exophthalmic brown eyes that study me curiously. And why not? I am the first woman her 26-year-old brother has brought home to her house, and she is eager to inspect the package.

We shake hands awkwardly as Hal carries our bags into the house, with its flowery chintz slipcovers, Noguchi coffee table, and Hans Wegner Danish Wishbone chairs. Victoria brings in trays of snacks — hot tea, pistachio nuts, then brie and crackers and red wine. Still later, she fills our glasses with Perrier. It is cold in the house, and I am getting hungry. But Rick's sister and brother-in-law don't seem to be making dinner. Hal lights a joint. I don't smoke with them. I can't take the chance of getting more paranoid than I already am.

"Where are the kids?" Rick asks. He is over six feet and handsome, his dark hair beginning to recede, pale, eager and much gentler than his sister.

"Spending the night with friends. They'll be home tomorrow morning." Something is in the air. An unspoken excitement lights Victoria's eyes. Hal taps his fingers against his thigh, then runs upstairs and returns with a silver box and a small green slab of marble. "Surprise," he says. "My sound man came through. Ready for some lines?"

Lines? I glance at Rick. I think this means cocaine. I have never had cocaine. I'm not eager to experiment with a new drug in this foreign setting, and Rick doesn't seem thrilled either.

"Will I hallucinate?" I whisper to Rick.

Victoria has heard me. "You'll love it, Jill. It's nose candy. A happy time."

"Geeze, Victoria," Rick says, shaking his head. "What about dinner?"

"Later, little brother," Victoria says. "We'll go out." Hal is showing us how he chops up the little white chunks into a powder with a razor blade. Then he sniffs it through a straw.

"Come on, you two." Victoria pulls me down on the sofa. "It's really pure."

I'm the last to sniff the white powder off the little green slab. The bare branches of a tree scrape against the windows. Rick shrugs in my direction as Hal leads him off somewhere to show him the tape of an ad he's just finished for a suitcase company.

Victoria and I have moved to the loveseat in the sunroom adjoining the living room. There's a sour taste in the back of my throat, but so far I don't feel anything, which is a relief. I do notice that chatting with Victoria becomes surprisingly easy. After a few minutes, or perhaps an hour, we are gliding together in a riveting conversational fugue that builds, relaxes, and builds again. Her perfume is overpowering, something to do with daffodils and lilacs. I feel suddenly articulate, even brilliant. She is brilliant, too, and very different from Rick, who often speaks haltingly, as if he has prepared what he's going to say long before he opens his mouth. What am I talking about with Victoria? Watergate? The sailboat they keep in Long Island Sound? Her children, eleven and nine? I can't say exactly, but it doesn't matter. I am feeling Victoria's essence in my legs and my chest, which is tingling now. Should I be worried? What if Victoria has awakened in me the longing and excitement I am hoping to feel for Rick? When she touches the back of my hand, I cannot find my breath, or my brain.

"Victoria? Jill?" I am startled to see Rick standing in the doorway, studying us quizzically. "It's getting late. Let's go eat." I look at my watch. It's 11 p.m. I haven't eaten since noon. I must be hungry, but it's hard to know.

"We've got to go, Vic," Hal says, "or everything will be closed."

The backseat of the Jaguar smells of leather and Victoria's perfume. We are searching White Plains and Rye and other nearby towns I've never heard of to find a place to eat. Everything *is* closed — their two favorite Italian, the Mexican, the Thai, and even the last-ditch Chinese take-out. Hal and Rick are in the front seat, and Hal is irritable now. He swings by the Kentucky Fried Chicken, but it has also closed. We drive back home. Hal and Rick are tired. I glance at Victoria, who glances at me, then looks away. I am not tired at all, just cold and slightly numb.

Hal and Victoria have already asked Rick discreetly if we are sleeping together, and since we aren't, Victoria leads me into a bedroom on the second floor belonging to their daughter. It is a large and pretty room, neat and pink, with pinups of David Cassidy and Marie Osmond on the walls, pink-quilted twin beds, and a pink dressing table with matching chair. Rick will sleep in Harry's room down the hall. We say good night on the landing, halfway up the stairs. "How are you doing?" Rick whispers.

"OK, I think."

"Victoria likes you. She told me in the kitchen."

"She's entertaining," I say. "I feel kind of wired."

"That's the cocaine," Rick frowns. "Sorry about that." Rick yawns. "Victoria exhausts me. I told you she was crazy. Now you know."

Victoria is staring up at us from the bottom of the stairs, head cocked to one side. "What are you saying, little brother?"

Rick laughs. "We were saying how much we love you, Victoria."

"And I love you," his sister winks.

In the pink bed in the daughter's pink sheets, I lie awake, unable to sleep. Rick's sister and brother-in-law seem slightly off-kilter, not eating food, only drinking tea and wine and snorting cocaine. I wonder what Rick and Hal were doing all the time I talked to Victoria. They were supposed to be looking at a video, but I wonder if they were having sex. Sometimes two men can have sex very quickly, Rick has told me. Even if they're straight. Just because they can. No strings attached. And Rick really admires Hal for having his own ad agency and making a ton of money. But somehow I don't think even Rick would have sex with his sister's husband while she and I are in the next room. I'm being insecure. I inhale, count backwards from one hundred to zero twice, taking comfort in the clean smell of the sheets and the stillness of this big suburban house, so different from my noisy one-room studio on an alley in downtown Philadelphia.

The clock strikes two A.M. I hear a noise. Someone is at the door. A figure tiptoes toward me in what looks like a large overcoat.

"Jill? You awake?" It's Victoria. She sits down on the bed. The feel of her body next to mine awakens an ancient, unmentionable hunger.

"Listen," she says softly. "I want to take you for a ride in the Jag."

"What?"

"The Jaguar. Don't get dressed, just put on your coat."

I stare at her dark shape. "Now?"

"Why not? You won't be able to sleep."

My heart lurches. I want to go, but Victoria is crazy, Rick says. She could take me over the edge if I'm not careful. I pull off the covers.

"Don't get dressed, Jill. Just wear your coat."

I find my jeans and a sweater. I'm way too uptight to go driving around naked. The stairs creak as we tiptoe down to the kitchen. My hands are sweating. What if Hal and Rick hear us?

Victoria is already in the garage revving her Jaguar and is indeed naked, save for her fur coat. I can see her breasts as she reaches up to click her Magic Genie remote-control garage door. She drives very slowly, toward Long Island Sound and is talking non-stop, mesmerizing me as she slows for a stoplight. The light changes from green to red, then back to green and red again, but Victoria does not move the car.

"Shouldn't you drive?" I say.

"I'd rather talk to you."

"You're not worried about the cops?"

She shrugs. "I know most of them." I don't ask why. Suddenly, she presses her foot onto the accelerator and roars off the big road onto some back road and up to what seems to be a cove, where she lurches to a stop. We sit in the dark overlooking the ocean. Or maybe it's Long Island Sound. I don't know the geography here. She is talking about Rick. "He's gay, you know."

This is the first mention of anything gay all evening. It is a step in the direction of my craving, and I'm relieved and eager to finally get there.

"I don't understand my brother," she is saying. "Or what two men see in each other. But I can understand two women being, you know, attracted."

I inhale and grip the door handle. I feel the heat of her words. "I can, too."

She leans closer. On the radio, Roberta Flack is singing "Killing Me Softly."

We sit in silence, the November air chilling me to the bone, the tension screaming between us. "I am attracted to you, Jill," Victoria whispers.

The cocaine is racing inside me again, but I do not feel brilliant anymore, just excited and weird. I have never been this close to a woman. I have stuffed down my feelings since first grade, never allowed myself any expression of my sexual attractions to women. I have been with a dozen men but never kissed a woman. And here, next to me, is my boyfriend's sister, her arm around my shoulders, her lips so close I can smell them. I play with the zipper of my jacket. "I've never... not with a woman."

Her breath singes my neck. "Really?"

"Really." Roberta Flack croons softly with her songs. I want to pull Victoria close, write my name across her naked torso. "I've wanted to. A lot. Be with a woman."

"Hal thought you... were experienced," she says.

"Hal did?" I am blushing. I had not realized I was so obvious. I have worked so hard to keep my feelings bottled up.

Victoria is crawling along the streets again at five miles an hour. Her diamond engagement ring sparkles in the glow of the dashboard. "I find you very attractive, Jill."

I blush again, looking behind us in case a car might hear us talking, see us, stop us, arrest us. "I find you... attractive... too." The words creak out of my mouth.

She stops the car in the road again and fiddles with the stereo. Gladys Knight and the Pips boom "Midnight Train to Georgia" as she begins to stroke my hair. "Let's go home and go to bed, Jill."

Sirens roar in my brain. *Your boyfriend's sister? You're as crazy as she is if you do!* The electric clock ticks on the dashboard. "I would need a big drink first," I say finally.

She laughs. "Of course."

I have taken her hand and am kissing the tan, perfume-soaked fingers, amazed by my boldness. "I have wanted to do this," I whisper. My body is approaching meltdown. I am going to do it. I am kissing a woman. She guns the car and races back to her tree-lined street, magically opening the garage door.

In the kitchen, we grab glasses, filling two tumblers with Chivas Regal. We stand barefoot at the counter, gulping our drinks. The scotch burns, replacing the cold nerves of cocaine with the warm fire of alcohol and lust.

Victoria's eyes are shining, like Rick's do when he talks of the men he meets in the bars and bathrooms and the marsh near the airport. She leads me up the back stairs to her daughter's room. She takes off her coat, drops it on the floor, slides into the sheets. Since ages eight, twelve, fourteen and twenty, I have wanted to touch a woman. Each time I came close, I silenced the ache, shut off my desire, feared my family would disown me or a boss would fire me or God would electrocute me. And here I am, about to hold my boyfriend's sister, who is waiting for me in the bed. She opens her arms as I hesitate, then press myself against her long, fit body. The feel of her skin against mine wobbles my heart. She is filling me with flowers, with roses and gardenias, with a lover's dream. Her hips move; I am feeling the heat of her. I am handling her. I am *Gunsmoke's* Matt Dillon lassoing Miss Kitty; I'm a sailor in *South Pacific* dancing with Mary Martin; I'm Gene Kelly with Debbi Reynolds singing in the rain. Victoria allows me, urges me to move on top of her. "I want you, Jill," she whispers. "I want you!"

"I want you, too," I say. Did I really say that? Did she? Or am I imagining these things I have craved so long? The scenes in my head are all of men and women in the movies. Is that weird? I have never seen two women falling in love on a movie screen or in real life.

This is better than the movies; I'm fairly sure it is actually happening. For a moment, I forget the teachers and teammates and movie stars I have loved from a distance. They were all off-limits, dangerous and thrilling.

"What is that smell?" I ask. "Like toothpaste."

She laughs. "Femme Unique."

"What's that?"

"Vaginal deodorant."

Vaginal deodorant? I have never smelled vaginal deodorant before. I kiss her thighs, brush my cheek against her legs. Something bristles on my lips.

"I shave there," she whispers. She shaves her legs all the way up to her pubic bone. Perhaps this is what suburban women do. They shave and wear deodorant everywhere. How strange. How unique.

She sleeps in my arms after she comes while I lie awake, savoring this pressure of her head upon my shoulder, the heat of her breath against my cheek, the smell of her sweat and my pussy. She is Patricia Neal, Jean Seaberg, Sophia Loren, Greta Garbo. She is my lover and my wife. I do not want this night to end.

We are breast to breast when the dim early light creeps through the curtains. Against the pink sheets, Victoria's face seems older and more solemn this morning. She looks at me with a sadness I did not see when we were coked up in her car. Maybe it was there last night, but I don't know. We begin again, pressing and throbbing and kissing, making sure this is not a dream. We both come and fall back to sleep,

"Victoria?" A man's voice. We jerk up. Hal is standing in the doorway, unshaven, handsome, bare chested, in blue jeans. "Get up, Victoria. The kids will be home in fifteen minutes." He studies us, wound in each other's arms, and closes the door.

I notice an African doll in a woven headdress propped up on her daughter's bookshelf. "Is Hal mad?"

"Hal? He shouldn't be." She stretches languidly, then snuggles down into my arms. "This was his idea."

"His idea?" She is so close to me that she has three eyes.

"He wouldn't have sex with me last night but he said he thought you might be interested."

I swallow, loosening my grip on her waist. "This was your husband's idea?"

She kisses my ear. "A good one, don't you think?"

"Very good." I stare at her fur coat in a pile on the floor. "But I thought you were attracted to me."

"I am. I was." She kisses my cheek. "Don't let go of me."

I hold her tight again. I search for words. "You wanted to, didn't you, Victoria?"

The door opens again. Hal has shaved and is fully dressed now. "Get the fuck up, you two. The kids are downstairs." He slams the door.

Victoria closes her eyes, opens them, inhales, rises, and stands naked in front of me.

"I miss you already," I say. And it is true. I feel like crying.

"You're adorable." She picks up her mink coat and leans over to kiss me. "You're sure you've never done this before?"

I shake my head. "First time ever."

"It was fun, wasn't it?"

"Very," I say. "I'd like to do it again."

"Again and again and again and again." She blows me a kiss and closes the door behind her.

I lie there, afraid to move, afraid to disturb this delicious mesh of scents and feelings. Someone knocks on the door. Please, let it be Victoria, coming back for more, and not her daughter. The door opens. Rick's brown eyes are wide, his smile eager. He wears a blue-and-white striped button-down shirt and pressed blue jeans.

"Guess what?" I smile.

"What?" He sits next to me on the pink bed that Victoria has just vacated. The feeling is so different. There is no electric shock, no breathless freefall, no molecular dissolve.

"Try to guess," I grin, sitting up, pulling the covers over my breasts.

"I can't guess." There are shadows under his eyes. The cocaine must have kept him awake, too.

"Victoria and I were lovers." It is hard to say now that I have said it.

His eyes widen. "What?"

"We... did it."

"Did what?"

I pull the covers higher. "She took me for a ride in her car, and we talked about you, and talked and talked and drank scotch and then we..." I hesitate. "We made love. We got it on."

"You got it on?" His eyes widen. He stands up. "Goddamn, Victoria." His back is to me now as he clenches his fists. "Fucking A."

"What's wrong?"

"What's wrong?" He shakes his head. "My sister always has to be top dog. She just *has* to get the better of me. It's her thing. She can't resist."

I have never felt so happy in my life. "Do you know what this means, Rick? I've broken through. I'm over pretending. I'm on my way."

He faces me, color drained from his cheeks. "She did it to hurt me, Jill," he says, hovering grimly above me, wringing his hands. "To hurt me and Hal."

"Hal suggested it," I say.

"Oh, sure," Rick says. "If Hal suggested it, he was pissed at her."

I close my eyes. I thought last night had to do with me and Victoria and not some sort of family power struggle. I thought we were two people, two women, hungry for each other, for sex with each other, for the forbidden. The ecstatic. "It didn't have anything to do with you and Hal."

"You don't know her." He slams the door behind him.

In the kitchen, all six of us — the two kids, Victoria, Hal, Rick and I — eat bagels and cream cheese, orange juice, and coffee around the rectangular table, set with yellow French provincial placemats and napkins. The children steal shy looks at me. Hal does not speak; his eyes are fixed on the *New York Times*. I glance at Victoria, who avoids my eyes. Her daughter is telling Rick about the bowling party she went to yesterday, where one of her friends ate so many hot dogs she threw up, and it was hysterical, and they had a wonderful time. It is strange, this change in Victoria. She is distant and watchful now. Is Rick right? Did she have sex with me to hurt Rick and Hal, who is already clearing the dishes? Victoria glances at me with curious eyes, letting just a trace of last night show in them. But they go dull again when Hal asks if she has called the electrician about rewiring the fuse box. Her face has tightened into a mask.

Rick looks at his watch and then me. "We should get going, Jill. I've got a four o'clock meeting." For some reason, I wonder if it is a sex hook-up. He has a lot of those.

"On Sunday?" Victoria stares at him and stands up. "Cool your jets one second, baby bro. I want to show Jill the garden." She pushes away from the table and takes my hand.

"Do it fast," Rick growls, looking at his watch. Hal and Rick and the kids carry our bags to the car while Victoria and I roam their large back garden, arm in arm. There is so much I want to say. We walk as far as we can, to the bed by the far green hedge, where we spot a pale blue hydrangea that has somehow survived the November cold.

"Thank you," I say, squeezing Victoria's hand.

She glances at the house. "Rick's furious."

"He'll forgive you." I smile into her worried eyes, trying to reassure her. *I love you. We are married*, I try to say with my expression.

"I've fucked up again." Her jaw clenches the way Rick's sometimes does when he talks about his mother, who lives in the same building and often stops by his apartment uninvited. "Everything seems so hopeless," she sighs. "Rick and Hal are always angry at me — no matter what I do." *Getting in bed with me was probably not the greatest idea*, I think, *if you were worried about keeping your brother and husband happy.*

Near us, a robin pecks the hard ground looking for a worm. "If they knew how wonderful we felt, maybe they wouldn't be so mad," I say.

She cocks her head to one side. I see the beginning of a smile. "It was fun, wasn't it?"

"Extremely fun," I grin. "I wish we could go upstairs right now." I want to ask her to come to Philadelphia. Or to meet me in New York. "I'd love to spend a whole night and a day with you." She does not answer. She feels the children, Rick, and Hal staring at us from the kitchen window, then glances at me, hesitates, and kisses me on the lips. Turning, she snaps off the head of the pale blue hydrangea.

Rick roars out of Rye. He cannot get away fast enough. He doesn't want to hear about Victoria and what happened last night, but I tell him anyway. I want so much for him to understand what's happened. As a gay man, I think surely he understands. My molecular structure has changed, undergone a complete transformation after a lifetime of repression. The world feels different. Even the littered on-ramps of the New Jersey Turnpike and the acrid skyline of Newark look glorious. I have done it. I have made love with a woman. I have lost my virginity. I am free. I am alive. I am alive!

For days, weeks I move in a dream. I think only of Victoria, of her body, her voice, her suburban lair, her Jaguar. I write her a thank-you note.

"Don't write Victoria," Rick tells me one night at dinner.

"Why not?" I say, surprised.

"She doesn't want to hear from you."

"She doesn't?"

"Leave her alone, Jill."

"Why? What's happened?"

Rick won't say.

Despite his anger and my new lesbian status, Rick and I become lovers. He is a kind, considerate lover. But he is not his sister. We will never float and coast in a sea of roses or get hot just sitting near each other. But sex with him seems, inexplicably, like a necessary step in the process of my coming out. The next step is even bigger. I land a job in New York so my life as a lesbian can begin in earnest. I keep hoping I'll see Victoria on the street in New York, that she will call me and we'll meet at the Plaza or run into each other in Midtown, near my company, and fall into each other's arms.

Rick moves to New York a few months after I do, but our affair is over. My transformation is almost complete. I am in love with New York and a lesbian bar called the Duchess at Sheridan Square and a beach on Fire Island where I have sex with a woman I meet at the Second Annual Lesbian/Gay Pride Parade.

Six months later, by the Seventy-second Street IRT, I run into Rick as he is buying the *New York Times* at a kiosk near the entrance. "Rick?" He turns and smiles. We talk for a while; he tells me about the film he is making for public television and about Steve, his new love.

With hesitation, I ask, "How's Victoria?"

He wipes something from his eye. "Don't ask."

"What's wrong?" I say.

"She's had a total breakdown."

"Breakdown?" I swallow. A homeless man is peeing on the sidewalk.

Rick's brown eyes, the eyes of a skeptical friend now, not a lover, assess me slowly, then decide to trust me again. "She flipped out. Ran naked through Rye with a knife screaming that Hal was trying to kill her. When the police picked her up she told them he'd been holding her hostage in the garage. It wasn't true, of course. Probably too much cocaine and God knows what other drugs." Rick pauses as a bus rumbles down Seventh Avenue. "She's locked up now, in a closed ward. Thank God for Thorazine. She's a zombie but she's stable."

"I'm so sorry." I take a breath.

A Great Dane with an enormous pink tongue is licking a child's ice cream cone that has fallen into the gutter. As an afterthought, Rick adds, "The children are with Hal's parents for now. After that, who knows?"

My head is exploding. "I'm sorry," is all I can manage.

"Me, too." He bites his lip.

"Can I write her? Call her? Do you have her address?"

He squints down at some broken glass near his feet. "That wouldn't be good," he says. "A letter from you might, you know, upset her."

"Excite her," I whisper, fading slowly down into the underground.

NOT QUITE LIKE US

Until that time, my only memory of Philadelphia was a childhood climb through the throbbing walls of an enormous pink heart at the Franklin Institute. That rubbery, pulsing heart took my breath away. Because of it, I knew, when my parents told me they were moving to Philadelphia, that Philadelphia was more exciting than Baltimore, where the only memorable attraction was Fort McHenry and the Bromo Seltzer tower that sometimes lit up blue at night.

I visited my parents' new home for the first time on spring break from college in 1967, when I got a ride with a sophomore named Arnold, who lived in Atlantic City, a place with some really weird and interesting attractions, like a Boardwalk with a giant tusked elephant made of one million pieces of wood and a mechanical Planters' Peanuts man dressed in a top hat and tapping on the store window with a small baton. Arnold assured me I'd like the downtown neighborhood my parents had chosen, four blocks from the Liberty Bell and Independence Hall.

It felt strange to knock on my parents' door like a guest. It was a new row house in a row of identical row houses kitty-cornered from an ancient osteopathic hospital where I would soon buy Tareyton's from the cigarette machine late at night, when the drug store nearby was closed. My parents had the same furniture, the same overstuffed couch and easy chairs, the same silver cigarette box and candle sticks and inlaid sideboard they'd had in Baltimore, but everything else was new — the upholstery, the appliances, the green wall-to-wall carpet. I liked new. It was a nice change from our house in Baltimore, where everything was a little run down and sticky in the summer heat.

The rooms in the narrow house were small. Imitation Hollywood stage lights surrounded the bathroom mirrors, and the counters were white Formica. Late at night, especially on weekends, I could hear horse-drawn buggies clattering over the cobblestones carrying tourists toward Independence Hall. In this new life, my mother served wine with dinner, on top of cocktails, becoming more argumentative with each glass. Because of my father's job, they traveled a lot, staying in big hotels around the country. In all three bathrooms, my mother placed little shoeshine kits and small bottles of soap and shampoo and moisturizer she'd picked up at those hotels.

In this new city, my parents made new friends. Like themselves, many of their downtown neighbors had moved there because of their work. Others arrived from the suburbs of Philadelphia after their children had grown.

"They're not quite like us," my mother would say of some of the neighbors. "But we're creating a community. And community is vital to everyone's sense of belonging and well-being." My mother, a trained social worker, had recently learned about "hang-ups" and "blocks" and "breakthroughs" at an encounter group her beloved Reverend Smiley in Baltimore facilitated for some of the groovier members of his church. Determined to let down some of her "barriers," Mother had made a few new friends in Philadelphia who had never gone to boarding school or stayed up until three A.M. at debutante balls dancing to Lester Lanin. One of those new friends was a journalist; another was a gynecologist from Wisconsin; a third was the wife of a hospital executive from North Carolina. Her name was Labelle.

Labelle Goodwin will always remain indelibly linked in my mind to my first experiences in Philadelphia. She was a tiny woman (a strange thing in my family of giants), Southern, and pretty. She chain-smoked and wore her silver hair in a short page boy. She was in love with her malamute dog named Zoot. Zach, her husband, matched her perfectly. He was also short and Southern and a chain-smoker. Both were passionate readers. They did not read books on liberation theology, like my mother, or on science and medicine, like my father. They read *novels.* And they watched TV.

Reading novels was not an acceptable activity in my family; my parents would no more lounge in a La-Z-Boy reading John Updike than they would spend an evening playing Pee-Wee golf. Nor would they own an impractical dog like an Alaskan malamute that needed to be groomed and walked twice a day. Our dog was a beagle mix named Peter that my mother had accidentally lost when she let him out the back door in Philadelphia, just as she had in our quieter neighborhood in Baltimore. Peter never came back, but my mother didn't seem too concerned about losing him. He didn't fit into her new life of travel and community. Something else about my parents — they did not listen to music. If someone foolishly gave them a record album, my father opened the China closet and pulled out my old record player – gramophone, Dad called it — and listened to the tinny sounds long enough to get the gist. Then he'd put it away and make a note in his vest-pocket planner to send the giver a thank-you note.

Labelle and Zach lived six houses away, in a living room identical to my parents', where they reclined side-by-side in their La-Z-Boys, chain-smoking, playing their stereo and reading brand new hardback novels from Robin's Bookstore. Very often, after dinner, they might watch *Laugh-In* or *Ironside* or *The Fugitive*, something not done at my parents' house. Mom and Dad only watched the *CBS Evening News* with Walter Cronkite during cocktails. After dinner, Mom mended clothes and made calls for the North Philadelphia settlement house on whose board she served while my father read medical journals and reviewed case notes.

Over the years, when I visited my parents, my mother would invite their new friends over for dinner, but never Labelle and Zach. I didn't understand why. Labelle Goodwin was whimsical and Southern and comfortable with eccentric people, whether from books, TV, movies, or real life. Everyone was OK, particularly if their stories were entertaining. Labelle never asked why I did not have a boyfriend and did not seem to think it odd that I wasn't as current on contemporary TV as they were. She loved to tell me about their favorite *Laugh-In* skits as their two sons, both a little younger than I, suntanned and handsome, would hurry through the living room on the way to their rooms or to their jobs as lifeguards and parking valets at Bookbinders. I envied their cocky sways and unselfconscious sense of male entitlement.

The first time I visited Labelle by myself, without my mother, was sometime in the summer of 1967. She gave me a glass of sweet tea, offered me her husband's La-Z-Boy, and told me about a young friend of hers from North Carolina who had recently made a record album and was on his way to becoming famous. Had I ever heard of James Taylor?

No, I hadn't.

Labelle leaped up and dropped a James Taylor record onto her high fi. The tune was "Carolina on My Mind." His sweet voice and guitar and lyrics were so hopeful and poignant they made me feel freer than I had in ages. Labelle lit another cigarette.

"I love that boy," she said. "I love that whole family. His daddy's a doctor. Worked at Zach's hospital. So did his granddaddy. They've had a terrible time. They're all smart as whips and musical and drink a little too much, more than what's good for them. But James will be a household name someday. He's on his way."

As I walked home, I felt ready to face my parents six houses away, where the vibes weren't as warm and where I *was* expected to have boyfriends and goals for my life and a clear idea of how I would support myself until I married... a man, of course.

In 1973, after college and graduate school and two desperate years working in a bookstore in Philadelphia, the closet was killing me. I moved to New York, where there were jobs and lesbian bars and so much more. My first weekend there I marched in a gay and lesbian pride parade. Three months later, in the dunes of Fire Island, ocean pounding behind us, sun high above, I made love with an index editor from Scribner's. My life changed. I went to women-only bars, had lesbian friends, and began to feel very nearly happy.

A year later, I took an Amtrak down to Philadelphia with Margo, my lover, to tell my parents I was a lesbian. It did not go well. My mother, temporarily forgetting the importance of self-actualization and self-disclosure, was devastated, particularly, it seemed, by the idea that I would not be producing a grandchild. Those were the days before lesbian parenting was commonplace. Having narrowly escaped the torments of the closet, I was not tempted by the prospect of producing an heir on which my mother could dote.

My mother's face lightened a little when I proposed taking Margo to visit Labelle.

"Oh, do, Jill," said my mother. "Labelle will be thrilled. She adores you."

Labelle made Margo feel more welcome than my mother had, giving us beer and potato chips and telling us her news of James Taylor, now married to Carley Simon. Margo did thrill Labelle when she confided that she knew Carley's brother Peter, a photographer whose book cover she'd designed.

"Labelle likes your... *friend* very much," my mother said the next morning, closing the *New York Times*. Margo was upstairs in bed reading, afraid to come down. "Said she was tremendous." My mother wiped away tears.

"I'm so glad," I said, pouring myself some coffee.

"Labelle says you're a great girl, Jill. Always tells me not worry about you. 'Jill's fine,' she says. 'You should be very proud.'"

"Did you tell her?"

"Tell her what?"

"That Margo and I are lovers."

My mother looked startled. "Of course not. That's private."

I sighed. "Do you ever have them over?"

My mother hesitated. "They're not... Zach's... not a doctor. I adore Labelle, of course." She sighed. "But not for dinner."

"Why not? They're both so smart and warm."

"Don't hate me, Jill." Mom glanced at the thin black book on top of the huge Philadelphia telephone book sitting on the kitchen counter.

"They're not *Social Register*?"

My mother nodded. "But I adore her. What time does your friend get up?"

"Her name is Margo, Mom."

Two years later, my mother phoned — it was a Tuesday, not her usual Sunday call. Margo and I had decided to move to California. "Horrible news," my mother said. "Labelle's in the hospital." Some people, even friends, you're kind of thrilled to hear bad news about. But not Labelle. Never Labelle.

I took a breath. "What's wrong?"

"She's unconscious."

"What?" I closed my eyes. I could see Mom leaning over the Formica kitchen table in the not-quite-as-new row house.

"She had a cold, and then a splitting headache. A really bad one. Zach took her to the ER, and the next thing we knew, she was unconscious. They think it's spinal meningitis, which Dad says is a terrible disease." My mother's voice was tight. "I've visited. She looks fine. So pretty, as always, like her old self, but she doesn't wake up, doesn't know anyone, can't talk or understand, just lies there, asleep or unconscious, I'm not sure which. It's terrible to see. Zach lives at the hospital."

Every Sunday for a month, Mother reported on Labelle. Still alive, still in a coma. Then one Sunday, "Labelle died yesterday."

I blinked. "No."

"She never woke up."

"I'm so sorry."

"She always said you were a great girl."

"She was a great woman," I said, wiping an eye.

"Zach's a... widower now." Mother was practicing the words, trying to come to grips.

"How are the boys?"

"They'll be here a while — to help Zach." My mother inhaled. "Do you really have to move to California?"

"Margo's starting a new job there."

"Why do *you* have to go?"

"She's my partner, Mom. We're a couple."

"But California? It's so far away."

"But there are airplanes. I'll come back." The truth was, I was worried about moving to California myself. I loved New York, and I would miss the Village, and our community of lesbian friends, and the hair salon on Bleecker Street where we all got shorn, and Mother Courage restaurant owned by two women we knew, and all the shops on Barrow and Bedford and West Fourth streets. But I couldn't tell my mother that, and I couldn't tell Margo. I was going to try California and life as a lesbian far from home and the sizzle of Manhattan.

"San Francisco is so far away," my mother said again. My coming out had been crushing for her. She still dreamed of those grandchildren and me marrying a man. I wanted so much to make her happy, but I felt lucky to be alive and have someone I loved, and who loved me. I wanted that be enough for her. To be enough for me.

"You can always come live here with us if it doesn't work out," she sighed. I was crying, but she didn't know it. "You come home and live with Daddy and me. Your room on the third floor will always be here. We love you so much."

Seven years later I did come home from California to my room on the third floor in Philadelphia. My mother had found a malignant lump in her neck, and a year later, her surgeon removed a far bigger tumor from her rectum. She had four operations and chemo and radiation. Her hair fell out and she wore a wig and could barely walk. When there was nothing else the surgeons and oncologists could do to stop the cancer, she came home in an ambulance to her mahogany bed in her boxed-shaped bedroom in Philadelphia.

Mother never talked about dying, even as the oxygen machine chugged by her bedside, and my father changed her colostomy bag, and I rubbed lotion on her thirsty skin. Her friends – the old ones from Baltimore, the newer ones from Philadelphia – came to see her, their faces tight and sad, eyes red from tears, as she talked of her plans to "beat" the cancer.

Close to the end, when Mom choked and coughed and gulped for air, I imagined Labelle, once six doors down, now in heaven, waiting to open the pearly gates for my mother. Small and lively and so very Southern, Labelle would reach out with that twinkly smile, pour my mother a drink, fill a bowl with potato chips, and tell her that I was a great girl. Then she'd play James Taylor on her hi-fi as Mom leaned back in Zach's La-Z-Boy, enjoying her bourbon and those sweet songs and Labelle's saga of the Taylor family, who were so smart and artistic and talented, and who were, in fact, very much like them, like Labelle and Zach, like Mom and Dad, like the debutantes and down-and-out families at the settlement house where my mother volunteered. They all drank a little too much and were very, very complicated.

WHAT TO DO WHEN YOU FEEL TRAPPED

The silence was killing her, and she did not know what to do. After dinner, Jill opened another bottle of the chardonnay they had taken to ordering by the case. *Say something,* Jill told herself as Margo scraped fish bones into the garbage can. "We need to talk."

Margo's blue eyes looked startled. She turned off the faucet. "That sounds serious."

"Everything's fine," Jill said. *I feel trapped,* she thought. Margo folded her striped apron and sank onto the living room couch that turned into a king-sized bed for houseguests, mostly friends of Margo's, who'd been visiting from New York non-stop since their move to San Francisco the year before. Margo placed her wine glass on one of the handsome French end tables she'd bought at an antique store on Bedford Street in Greenwich Village. Most everything in their flat was Margo's, from her spacious two-bedroom on Hudson Street. Jill had sold her bed and two director's chairs to the woman who'd taken over her lease when she'd moved to Margo's from her walk-up on Eleventh Street.

Margo's dachshund, Dorothy, leapt on to the couch, looking uncertainly from Margo to Jill and opting to curl next to Margo.

"What's eating you?" Margo kicked off her leather pumps, tucking herself in the corner.

Jill's eyes fixed on the gold and lapis ring she had given Margo after their first year together, an acknowledgement of the relationship Jill had so feared and desired. *Say something*, Jill ordered herself. *Open your mouth*. "I think I'm depressed," she said finally.

In the silence, the drip of the guest toilet reminded Jill that she had not called Otto the plumber back as Margo had asked her to do. She'd lost half a day writing the last time the big, balding German made a house call. After announcing he did not have a toilet flapper on his truck, he'd ranted for two hours about a terrorist group that had recently murdered a German industrialist and hijacked a Lufthansa airplane, then said he would have to come back.

"I feel dead."

"What?" Margo stared at Jill.

"When we first got together, we talked about our childhoods, our crushes, our favorite movies, everything. Now we talk about whether to buy Fieldcrest or Ralph Lauren towels and who'll take Dorothy to the vet to refill her digitalis."

"I'll take her if you can't," Margo said, face reddening.

"No, I mean, I'll take her. That's not what I'm saying."

"We were *new*, Jill." Margo reached for Jill's hand as the western sun slanted through the bay windows onto her shoulder-length brown hair. "When you're new, everything about the other person is riveting. That doesn't mean we aren't still riveting, or we're dead, we've just... mellowed."

Margo was so lovely with her blue eyes, her high cheekbones, her round, sensual lips that reminded Jill of a movie star. Why had Jill come to feel so frozen around her? "In New York, we couldn't keep our hands off each other. We had sex nearly every night."

"We're not brand new, Jill," Margo laughed. "You can't have sirens every night."

Jill sipped her wine. "I've never been with anyone this long."

"What happened today?" Margo patted her hand. "Did someone in your writing group say something mean about your book? Is that what's upsetting you? Don't take what anyone says too seriously. Just keep writing. It's a first draft. Trust yourself."

"How can I trust myself if I don't think it's any good?"

"What you've read me is wonderful."

"Thanks."

"I'm not kidding."

Jill inhaled. Margo was unerringly supportive. "You're my best friend. You've given me a home and a dog and a life. I'm just..."

"We've made a life *together*, Jill. We've helped each other. If it weren't for you, I'd still be drinking a fifth of Scotch every night and dragging myself to work at noon, and you'd still be in your sooty little studio drinking cheap wine and picking up dykes at the Duchess."

"My apartment wasn't that bad," Jill frowned.

"It was a crash pad, not a home. And think of what we've accomplished, moving to California and getting the company to pay for both of us and landing this apartment and starting a new life. We're putting down roots in a new city. That takes time."

Jill sighed. "At least you have friends here."

"They're *work* friends, not soulmates, Jill. I miss New York, too, and Deena and everyone else. But, isn't it amazing that we're actually here in San Francisco, where the light is gorgeous, and our friends love to visit, and we can explore Yosemite and Big Sur and Point Reyes and fly down to L.A. if we want and see if Gail's sold her sit-com to Hollywood? That'll cheer you up. Maybe we should visit Gail."

Jill nodded. She didn't want to say what she was about to say, but it's what she felt, and she was trying to learn to express her feelings. "Have we become like an old married couple? You go to work, and I clean the house and walk the dog and spend a few hours doing nothing at the typewriter and have dinner ready when you get home."

"You're writing a novel!" Margo touched her arm. "That's not nothing."

"What if it comes to nothing?" Jill wished writing made her feel happier.

Margo shook her head. "Want to switch? I'll stay home and you go to work?"

"I'm unemployable."

"You're not."

Jill felt the grinding in her stomach. "I think we've become... like our parents." There, Jill had said it.

"*Your* parents," Margo winced. "I didn't have parents, remember?" Margo's father, a polo player from North Carolina, fell in love with Margo's mother at some big estate on Long Island where she was a chamber maid, fresh off the boat from Ireland, and he was a playboy. He'd left Margo's mother soon after Margo's little brother was born. "He'll be back," Margo's mother had promised her kids. But he never came back. He divorced Margo's mother, a sin and a scandal for a Roman Catholic, remarried, and sent an occasional check and a birthday card from North Carolina to Margo and her brother, while their mother supported the children as a clerk at the Hicksville Town Hall.

Margo poured more wine. "I'm sorry I'm not better company when I get home. It's the stress." She stroked Dorothy's head. "All of us at work are wrecks. We're starting a new publishing company in a new city where we don't know the printers or the suppliers or the authors or the freelancers. When I get home, all I want to do is lie on the couch and watch *Columbo* with you and Dorothy. It'll get better. I promise, Jill. Give it time. Give *me* time. Meantime, make some friends. If you had some friends you wouldn't expect so much of me."

"Should I have sex with these mythological new friends?"

"What?" Margo's eyes narrowed.

"We haven't had sex in weeks." Jill hated seeing the hurt in Margo's eyes. "You're always too tired or distracted or more interested hiking at Point Reyes or exploring tide pools than in lounging in bed on weekends the way we did in New York."

Margo stood up, paced to the kitchen, poured more wine, and sat back again, face red, nostrils flaring. "How can I feel sexy when they're driving me crazy at work with their deadlines and these flaky editors who don't give me the manuscripts until the day before the cover art is due. Then the marketing people get pissy because I don't have the mock-ups for the catalog, and the publisher says I'm paying my freelancers too much. And the paperwork, Jill, for one lousy freelance assignment, is ridiculous. Sometimes I think they want me to fail."

"I don't want you to fail," Jill whispered. "You're so good at what you do."

"If you really think sex will make you happy..." Margo stood angrily, cheeks flushed, unbuckling her brown leather belt. "Come on. Take off your clothes. Let's have sex. Right now."

Jill didn't budge. "I'm sorry I hurt your feelings. I don't want to. It's just, things seem..." She paused. "*Static* between us."

Margo shook her head. "That's rich, Jill. You feel *static* because you're not getting enough sex. But you're responsible for you own happiness, kiddo. If you're bored, make a friend. Go talk to somebody. Join the lesbian softball team. Take a class."

"I'm taking life drawing at the Art Institute."

"Take another class. Go out to lunch with someone from your writing group." Dorothy the dachshund eyed Margo nervously. She hated hearing them argue.

Jill inhaled. "All the women in my writing group are straight and much older than me, like a different generation."

"You don't have to *marry* them, Jill. Just have lunch. Talk about writing. Ask them about their lives. You're good at that."

Jill poked at her blue running shoe. "I miss dinners at Mother Courage and going to drinks with Deena at the Duchess and breakfast at the Bagel on Saturdays with Lizzie. I miss lesbians. I miss New York."

"There are no lesbians in San Francisco?" Margo shook her head. "What am I going to do with you? Maybe you should see that shrink someone told us about."

"I have." Jill chewed her lip.

"What?" Margo leaned forward. "And you didn't tell me?"

Jill shrugged. "She gave me a bataka bat and told me to pretend this big pillow was my father and to whack the pillow with the bat and yell, 'I hate you, Daddy,' to move energy into my pelvis."

"Jesus, Mother and Joseph!" Margo shook her head. "Your poor father. He is such a nice man. What about that woman in your art class who asked you to have coffee? Have you called her?"

Jill shrugged. "She's kind of weird."

"She doesn't have to be your best friend, Jill. Have coffee with her. Communicate. Reach out."

Jill gazed at the odd chandelier above the dining room table with the dusty glass prisms. "Maybe the chasm between you and me comes from our age difference."

"Chasm?" Margo reddened.

Jill forced herself to explain. "You came out as a lesbian in New York when you were eighteen and I was still in grade school memorizing multiplication tables. While you were sewing your wild oats with Deena and Lana and Sarah and God knows who else in New York, I was memorizing the causes of the Hundred Years' War. Seven years is a big difference."

"Six years," Margo said, standing up, then sitting down again. "I was born in 1941."

"Six years, then."

"I don't feel any chasm." She moved closer and put her arms around Jill. "I love you, Jill. What can I do to make you happy?"

Jill felt terrible. She loved Margo, but was she *in love* with Margo? What had happened to the magic? Weren't big, committed relationships like theirs also supposed to be sexy and exciting?

Margo stood up.

"Margo?" Jill reached for her hand. Margo headed to the kitchen. "What's wrong with me?"

Margo shook her head. "Nothing's wrong with you. You've moved to a new city, and you're at home alone all day, and I'm at work, and you need to make some friends. Just don't get one of your crushes. I can't handle one of your crushes."

Crushes. They were part of Jill's problem. When she got close to a woman, felt attracted enough to attempt a friendship, she fell in love with them, and that was torture.

———

The quiet studio at the Art Institute, where twenty students were drawing a man's muscular body with pencils and charcoal, soothed Jill's psyche. Their teacher was a funny, large, outgoing blond woman who laughed like Mama Cass and owned a gallery on Fillmore Street. Last week she'd told Jill her drawings had originality and a spontaneity she admired.

The hippie woman from Marin hovered next to Jill at the break. "You going to have coffee with me at Vesuvio's?"

"Now?" The woman smelled of patchouli oil and cigarettes. The tassels of her leather jacket shimmied and moved like falling water. She had straight brown hair parted in the middle, bright, brown eyes, and a rib of flat, tanned skin that peeked like a hint of the Caribbean through the gap between her navy sweater and her long batik skirt. She wore flip flops and kept her multicolored, woven Guatemalan bag on her shoulder at all times, even when she worked.

"If we go now we can talk before Dean comes." The woman didn't move away.

"Class goes another hour." Jill looked at her watch.

"Are you taking this for a grade?" She glanced at the teacher. "She won't care. Come on."

"But I like this model."

"So do I. Let's go."

With Margo's caveat that she make a friend ringing in her ears, Jill packed up her supplies and walked with the hippie woman up Columbus Avenue, past a few leering North Beach drunks slung back on wooden benches, and up and over the hill to Vesuvio's, where they entered a long, narrow space with a dark bar and walls covered with painted murals of Beatniks in berets and blue jeans.

"I hope Dean's late," the woman said, ordering an Irish coffee. "He usually is." Jill ordered a mocha coffee.

Jill didn't know the woman's name and felt embarrassed to ask it. "What do you do?" she said, trying to relax, drinking her mocha.

The woman looked at Jill blankly.

"To support yourself?"

"Oh." She sipped her Irish coffee. "My old man has bucks."

"Your…"

"My father. What do you do?"

"Unemployment for two more months."

"Cool." She touched Jill's arm, "Also, I grow."

"Grow?" Jill stared at her.

"You know." She reached into her Guatemalan bag and pulled out a tin box. "I'm Vanessa, by the way."

"I'm Jill."

"I know." Vanessa opened the box to show Jill an array of hand-rolled marijuana cigarettes. Something about Vanessa, the way she spoke clearly one moment and in a kind of muffled, hypnotic whisper the next, reminded Jill of a novel someone in her writing group had recommended about an artist who could deconstruct and reconstruct himself cellularly, at will. Just disappear and reconstitute himself. Vanessa seemed to fade in and fade out like that; she was there, and then she was gone.

The cafe door opened. "Shit. Why is Dean here?" Vanessa waved to a handsome, unshaven guy with curly black hair and deep green eyes, a large nose, sweet smile and strong chin. He wore a white jean jacket over a green tank top, tan Levi's and dirty white sneakers. He held up a book from a large leather shoulder bag. "It's the new Ted Hughes," he said, grinning. He ordered an Irish coffee, lit a Camel cigarette and began reading one of the poems aloud.

"Dean, stop. Jill and I are talking." Vanessa looked down at her hands, trying to dig some dirt out from under one of her long, snaggly fingernails. "Do you garden, Jill?" Before Jill could reply, Vanessa's words burst forth like air expelled suddenly from a balloon. "My father was a financial genius in D.C. Set the interest rates for the Federal Reserve. Now he's drinking himself to death since my brilliant, crazy mother died. Ran naked through our penthouse until Daddio locked her up."

"Locked her up?" Jill interrupted, wide-eyed.

"At Saint Elizabeth's," Vanessa continued, slugging down her drink. "I was in college, dropped out before they threw me out, and married Elliott, whose draft status was One-A. When he shipped off to Vietnam, I fell in love with his best friend — Jack. Elliott nearly murdered us both when he got home so we divorced and I moved to

California, and my poor mother got lung cancer and died. And I'm writing a novel about all of them. Daddio bought me a house in Marin where I live with seven cats and three dogs."

"And me," Dean smiled pleasantly, looking up from his book of poems.

"And you, of course," Vanessa said, kissing Dean's cheek.

"Should be a great book," Jill said.

"It's mostly about my affair with Jack."

"What happened to Elliott?"

"He's in a mental hospital," Vanessa said squeezing Jill's hand. "What about you? Are you… "

"I'm writing a novel, too," Jill said. "Nothing as dramatic as yours. Two girls who get a crush on each other."

Vanessa looked at Dean. "I told you, Dean. Didn't I? I had a dream about this."

"You have so many dreams," Dean said, closing his book.

"Don't you remember?" Vanessa stared in disbelief at her boyfriend, then turned back to Jill. "Seriously. I dreamt you were writing a novel about two girls." Vanessa pressed Jill's hand.

Dean opened his book again, winking at Jill. "Don't ever ask Vanessa about her dreams. Unless you have about seven hours."

"Dean! That's mean!"

Dean smiled, removing a new book from his leather sack. "Listen to this. It's Galway Kinnell, called 'After Making Love We Hear Footsteps,' about a couple who discover their kids have heard them screwing."

"Did you buy that book or steal it?" Vanessa twisted a strand of hair around her index finger.

Dean shrugged. "Can't remember."

Vanessa sighed, turning to Jill. "Anyway…"

Jill noticed the clock behind the bar and stood up. "I've got to go."

Vanessa spilled Irish coffee on her blue sweater as she tried to pull Jill down. "Don't go. Where do you live?"

"Pacific Heights."

"We'll take you. Won't we, Dean? It's on our way."

"Sure." Dean smiled, carefully closing his leather bag.

Jill sat in the back of their Volkswagen van on a mattress piled high with clothes, tie-dyed scarves, wine bottles, books and empty Pepperidge Farm cookie bags. Dean lit a joint and passed it to Vanessa as he roared up Broadway by the old mansions, then braked hard, turning right onto Webster Street and stopping on the steep hill in front of Jill's building, a blue house halfway down Green Street.

"You live here?" Vanessa said as they idled. "The whole house?"

"The flat on the main floor, with the curved windows." Margo must have gotten home because the curtains were already closed. "Thanks for the ride. And the coffee."

"See you next week," Vanessa called from the window. "Let's have coffee again."

"Sure," Jill said, relieved to be home.

Margo was pouring kibble into Dorothy's bowl, still wearing her white silk blouse and tan slacks from work. "Where were you?"

"I had coffee with the woman from art class and her boyfriend. They drove me home."

"Congratulations." Margo kissed her cheek. "Why didn't you ask them in?"

Jill shrugged. "I don't think they're friend material."

"Friends don't have to fill your every need," Margo said, disappearing into the bedroom to change. "Just someone you can talk to."

"She did most of the talking," Jill said, lying down on the living room floor to pet Dorothy, who was wagging her tail, eager for a walk. "She had a crazy mother and an alcoholic father, and she's writing a novel about her affair with her husband's best friend while he was in Vietnam."

Margo appeared from the bedroom in shorts and a Harvey Milk T-shirt. "So what's the boyfriend like?"

"A poet. Friendly. Likes Galway Kinnell and Ted Hughes."

"He has good taste," Margo said.

———

The next Friday, Jill came directly home from art class and made zucchini lasagna and salad.

"No coffee with Vanessa today?" Margo said.

Jill shook her head. "She wasn't there."

Margo picked up Dorothy and kissed her ears. "Disappointed?"

Jill shrugged. "She's not quite right in the head."

Vanessa arrived late to art class the following Friday, her arms full of books. She walked right to Jill's easel and stared at Jill's sketch of the slender, white-haired female model sitting naked and cross-legged on a zafu pillow on the model's platform.

"I like it," Vanessa smiled, smelling of pot and patchouli oil. "How was last week?"

"Good. The model was a belly dancer. You'd have liked her."

"Darn."

"With tattoos."

Vanessa set up her sketch pad next to Jill's. "I wanted to come last week," she whispered, "but Dean announced he was going back to Villette, his drag queen who lives in a hotel on Stockton Street."

"Cool," was all Jill could think to say as Vanessa sketched with colored pens, her loose knitted halter top barely covering her suntanned breasts. Her blue skirt fell below her knees, and her hair was tangled, as if a family of gerbils had slept there. She was breathless and discombobulated. "He left at a terrible time because we've got so much to do in the garden. Plus, he makes the best mocha coffees in the world."

"Quiet, you two," the teacher called.

"Come to Vesuvio's?" Vanessa said as they packed up after class.

"Can't tonight." Jill looked at her watch. "We're having dinner with some friends of Margo's from work."

"Who's Margo?"

"My…" Jill hesitated. "My lover."

"Wow." Vanessa's brown eyes fixed on Jill's. "I want to meet her."

"Sure," Jill said, knowing Margo and Vanessa were not a match.

Margo, being older, had missed the hippie, anti-Vietnam, drug-taking-era completely.

Vanessa shrugged. "I brought you a Zora Neale Hurston novel called *Their Eyes Were Watching God*. Have you read it?"

"No."

"You'll love it. And *Flush*, Virginia Woolf's biography of Elizabeth Barrett Browning's dog. And *Sula*. I think it's Toni Morrison's best. What writers do you like?"

"I've got to catch the bus."

"Just tell me one."

"Joan Didion's *The White Album*?" Jill ran down the Institute steps toward the bus stop. "And *Portrait of a Lady*," she called as Vanessa ran to catch up with her.

"Henry James? Really? He puts me to sleep. What about *Orlando* and Lessing's *Golden Notebook?* Can't you come to Vesuvio's?"

"No."

"Then come to Marin next week. Do you have a car? I'll send Dean to Berkeley."

"I thought Dean moved back with the drag queen."

She laughed. "Villette's place is too small, and Dean missed our garden. And me. So he's back. What's your phone number? Come Tuesday."

"I write during the week." Jill squinted down Chestnut Street for the bus. She would have preferred to drive, but parking was impossible in North Beach. "I need to finish my novel before my unemployment runs out."

"You write every day?"

"Try to."

"Can't you take a day off?"

"Only for my writing group and drawing class."

"When do you see your friends?"

"I don't have any friends." The bus pulled up.

"What's your phone number?" Jill yelled out her number as she boarded the bus.

"I'll call you."

"Vanessa invited me for lunch in Marin next week," Jill said as they waited at The Dock in Tiburon to have dinner with Ricky and Earl. "Do you think I should go?"

Margo looked out at the sailboats on the Bay and the green hills of Angel Island. "How else are you going to make friends?"

They sat in a bubbling hot tub at Shabui Gardens in San Anselmo. Jill tried not to look at Vanessa's breasts, half in, half out of the water. Margo would definitely not approve of Vanessa, not one little bit. She was sexy and suntanned and weird, talking in her whispered, trance-like voice about Virginia Woolf and Vanessa Bell and her job at the Nixon White House.

"You worked for Richard Nixon?" Jill was astounded.

"I worked for Herb Kline, Nixon's speechwriter. I was one of those people sobbing on the White House lawn when the President flew off in the helicopter."

"I was clapping."

"I wasn't," she shrugged. "I know a lot of people were."

Was Vanessa telling the truth? "It's hard to see you writing speeches for Nixon."

Vanessa laughed, and when she did, her breasts lifted out of the hot tub. "It was a long time ago."

Jill did the math. Five years ago. Vanessa must have smoked a lot of dope to have changed so much in that time.

After the hot tub, Jill followed Vanessa up into the hills of San Anselmo, driving in her yellow Honda behind Vanessa's wheezing VW, through oaks and madrones and redwoods higher and higher, then taking a sharp right down a steep driveway to a rambling, brown-shingled ranch house hidden among gnarled coastal oaks and leaning bay laurels. Below the house was a swimming pool built into a large wooden deck where marijuana plants grew in brown cardboard pots and wine barrels and a white claw bathtub and a toilet bowl. Vanessa's cats tore around the grounds chasing three excitable border collies. It was a hippie pad, for sure, with wind chimes and stained-glass ornaments dangling from the tree limbs, and the decks in need of repair, and the gardens desperate for weeding. Possibly Dean wasn't doing quite as much gardening as Vanessa thought. The inside of the house was minimally furnished, with a frayed upholstered red sofa the cats had attacked and a fireplace and a formal dining room table and chairs that must have been left from Vanessa's married days. Glass doors opened on to a deck overlooking Vanessa's swimming pool and an old country club in the distance, where shrubs and high grass were overtaking two large, empty, fading turquoise pools.

The walls of the house were hung with colorful, unfinished, paintings of animals and flowers as well as naked women and men.

"Interesting," Jill swallowed.

"From my dreams," Vanessa said. "I have trouble finishing things. Something always seems to distract me. Dean says it's my greatest flaw."

The kitchen was sunny, with oak branches protecting the room from the western sun. The cupboards and chairs were painted royal blue, the shelves lined with jars of spearmint, comfrey, peppermint, tarragon and other herbs from the garden. Vanessa was definitely good at growing herbs.

She made coffee for them, pouring Amaretto into hers, and they sat on the deck staring down at the swimming pool.

"Dean will be gone all afternoon," Vanessa said. "He's selling used books on Telegraph Avenue and meeting Villette for coffee."

"I thought they'd broken up."

"He likes her blow jobs too much," Vanessa sighed. "But he'll come home. He always does."

After lunch of stuffed cucumbers, they lay in a lounge chairs on the deck, an afternoon breeze from the west cooling them.

"It's hard to imagine you at a preppy Southern college," Jill said, as Vanessa chain-smoked Marlboro's and described her childhood back East. "The girls I knew who went to your college were frighteningly normal."

"I was frighteningly normal once," Vanessa said.

Jill wondered about that. With her unshaven legs and batik gowns and pot smoking and literary references, she wasn't like any preppy Jill had ever known.

Vanessa stubbed a Marlboro into an abalone shell and lit a joint, offering it to Jill, who shook her head. "Makes me too paranoid."

"Really? It's sinsemilla. Grew it myself."

"Way too strong for me."

Vanessa looked disappointed. She inhaled a long drag. "I didn't want to go to Sweet Briar, but the college where my mother went turned me down. So I went to my fallback, hated it, dropped out and married Elliot. After we divorced, I moved to California and met Pete."

"What happened to Jack?"

"Oh, Jack," Vanessa laughed. "In real life, he fell apart. He's drinking himself to death. It's in my novel." She inhaled the joint, then put it in the abalone shell. "The good thing about Pete, and there wasn't a lot, was that he left the house at 4 a.m. to work at the stock exchange and played golf all the time, so he was never home. Which was good because he had a foul temper and bashed in the walls a few times. I was lucky it wasn't my head." She laughed. "When he punched me in the nose at the Washington Square Bar and Grill, Dean was there, saw the whole thing and took me back to his room with Villette. We've been together ever since."

"Wow."

Vanessa relit the roach. "Dean's sister is a jeweler, a really good one, and she moved in with us, and then she and I were together briefly, and then…"

"You and Dean's sister?" Jill laughed. "Dean didn't mind?"

"Dean encouraged us. Well, mostly he did." She shrugged and sipped the wine she'd poured. "Dean thought that to be a great writer in the tradition of Virginia Woolf I had to experience lesbian love. So Aurora and I became lovers, which was great until she stole some money from me and fell for a contractor in San Francisco and moved out."

Jill was feeling warm in the sun. "Dean didn't get jealous?"

Vanessa shook her head. "He doesn't believe in monogamy. Neither do I." She coughed hard.

"I think I'd better go," Jill said, looking at her watch.

Vanessa grabbed her hand. "But Dean won't be home for a while."

"But Margo will," Jill smiled.

"Tell me about Margo."

Jill looked at her watch. She told Vanessa about meeting Margo at their company in New York and moving to San Francisco last year.

"The charmed life," Vanessa said, staring down at the empty swimming pools. "I envy you."

Jill was puzzled. "You seem to have a good life. A house. Animals. A boyfriend who loves you."

Vanessa sighed. "Having just one dog and one lover and one book to write and one flat in Pacific Heights sounds lovely and uncomplicated to me. Magical, really."

"It has complications." Jill sighed, thinking of the dead, stifled feeling.

"Like what?"

"I don't have any friends."

Vanessa reached for her hand. "I'll be your friend."

Jill was not sure that was such a good idea.

"I wish you weren't so married." Vanessa said, her right arm now wrapped around Jill's shoulder, her lips next to Jill's cheek.

"But I *am* married," Jill said, feeling a surge of energy in her legs, the kind she'd experienced beating a pillow with a bat.

"Do you want to take a nap?"

"A nap?" Jill jingled the car keys in her pocket. "I have to go."

"Come lie down with me for a minute." Vanessa smiled an odd, crooked smile, running her fingers through her tangled hair as a cat whined from somewhere down below.

"Shut up, Tea Cake," Vanessa yelled. Taking Jill's hand, Vanessa led Jill into her bedroom, a dark cave with a huge brass bed made up with purple satin sheets and pillows. There was a brass hookah pipe in the far corner. The windows were draped with blue batik bedspreads.

"Take off your clothes," Vanessa said, stripping off her sarong. Her body was so dazzling Jill looked away.

Vanessa pushed Jill down, unzipping her jeans and pulling them off, tossing them in the corner. She unbuttoned Jill's shirt. "You're so beautiful," Vanessa said. "I knew you would be." She pressed Jill back onto the bed, wrapping her wrists and ankles with silk scarves, which she tied to the brass bedposts.

"What are you doing?" Jill tried to sit up.

"Isn't it obvious?" Vanessa laughed. She was a sight, with her suntanned body and her tangled hair, and now a large phallus hanging from a black leather belt she had strapped around her waist. She lay on top of Jill. "Play with me."

"Aren't you supposed to ask permission for things like this?" Jill said, alarmed. What would she tell Margo? Vanessa was pressing the phallus thing between her legs, moving it against her clit, anointing the phallus with a slippery goo from a plastic bottle as her hips thrust against Jill.

"Open for me," she whispered, plunging the probe inside Jill, one hand feeling Jill's breasts, the other hand guiding the phallus.

Jill had never liked men's dicks. She always felt too small and tight. But this one, big and unexpected, felt kind of good, and Vanessa's heat and smell and urgency aroused her.

"That's it, Jill," Vanessa whispered. "Let me fuck you."

Jill tried to move away but she was trapped.

Vanessa's mouth was on hers, her tongue deep inside, coaxing Jill as her prick began to sing, her hips thrusting rhythmically. "Come with me, Jill. Come!" she cried. They were breast to breast, hip to hip, Vanessa moving and sliding like a dancer, like a snake charmer, creaming Jill, exciting her, crawling up deeper.

"I like you, Jill," Vanessa whispered, moving her hand between her own legs, touching herself and rippling away. "I'm coming, Jill. I'm coming." Vanessa's vagina seemed to spill out over Jill, ejaculate in a way Jill had only experienced with men. Come was pouring out of her vagina, spraying over Jill's stomach and thighs. Jill could feel the walls inside her collapsing. "I'm coming," she cried. "So good."

They lay there, Vanessa on top, her plunger still inside Jill, her hips still moving slightly. They were skin to skin, breast to breast, lying dazed until the cats yowled and the dogs barked and the wind blew the oak branches against the windows. Vanessa withdrew, untied Jill and kissed her. Then they showered in Vanessa's lavender-tiled bathroom, transforming and re-forming so that Jill could drive home.

Margo opened the front door before Jill could throw off her jacket and feed Dorothy.

"How was your lunch date?" Margo folded her navy blazer on the couch and pulled some chicken breasts from the refrigerator. "Did you go to Vanessa's?"

"I did," Jill said, still dazed. "But first we went to a hot tub place near her house."

"What's her house like?"

"A hippie pad in the hills." Jill hoped she sounded normal. "She has seven cats, and three dogs, and lots of crazy paintings."

"And her boyfriend?"

"He was in Berkeley."

She looked at her watch. "You're home pretty late."

Jill hesitated. "Vanessa's quite a talker. Told me all about her novel and her life in Washington, D.C. She worked for the Nixon White House. Can you believe that?"

"She worked for Nixon?"

"Yes," Jill said, still shaken, trying to sort herself. "While you and I and everyone else drove with our lights on to protest the war, she supported Nixon and the war."

"Did she make you lunch?" Margo salt and peppered the chicken and thrust it into the broiler.

"She made cucumber boats."

"What?"

"Cucumbers sliced in half and filled with more cucumber and sesame seeds and vinegar and stuff."

"That's all? You must be hungry."

"I am." She should tell Margo the truth.

"And you talked? " Margo chopped some potatoes and threw them in a pot of water, not looking at Jill.

She talked, yes, and tied me up and fucked me. "She told me about Dean and his sister."

"But Dean was in Berkeley?"

"He was selling books with Villette."

Margo turned up the flame under the potatoes. "Will you see her again?"

"Class will be over in two weeks."

Dorothy had gobbled down her kibble and chicken and was pushing her bowl around the black and white linoleum tile floor with her nose, trying to lick out the last remaining crumbs.

"You OK?" Margo said, disappearing into the bedroom to change into her jeans. "You seem weird."

Jill followed her. If ever there was a time to tell the truth, this was it. "I stayed longer than I meant to. I'm sorry I'm late. She just kept talking."

"Maybe she really isn't friend material."

"Maybe she isn't." Jill leaned against the butcher block, afraid her legs might slip out from under her.

After dinner, in the middle of doing dishes, Jill put her arms around Margo's waist to steady herself. "I'm glad you're not crazy." She paused and pushed Margo's bangs away from her eyes. "How 'bout we lie down?"

"Now?" Margo said, surprised, sniffing Jill's hair. "What's that smell?"

"Probably the shampoo they use at the hot-tub place," Jill said quickly. She wanted to be held. She wanted to feel Margo close to her, to feel her sanity and love.

Margo followed Jill to the bedroom.

They had sex — gentle and familiar — for the first time in weeks.

Jill could not stop thinking about Vanessa but said nothing. She did not call Vanessa. Not the next day. Not the next month. Vanessa phoned many times, but Jill did not pick up.

"What should I tell her?" Margo would whisper if she answered the phone.

"Tell her I'm gone and you don't know when I'll be back."

"She sounds desperate."

"She's crazy," was all Jill would say. She missed Vanessa terribly.

A year later, Jill ran into Dean, who was sitting in an easy chair in the basement of City Lights reading poetry.

"Dean, is that you?"

"Jill?" He stood up and hugged her.

"How's Vanessa?" Jill said, trembling.

Dean, green eyes wide, his smile disarming, said, "She was mad at you for not calling. But she's happy now. Took off for the Caribbean and bought a sailboat there. She says she's pregnant."

"Pregnant?" Jill swallowed. "Congratulations!"

Dean shook his head. "It's not my baby. We haven't... not in months. Can I buy you a drink at Vesuvio's?"

Dean steered her into the bar and ordered them both a glass of red wine. "Her dad bought her a wooden boat, and I guess the baby's father came with it. She'll call you. She never lets go. She says she's coming back to have the baby."

"Wow," Jill said. "Do you still live at her house?'

Dean shrugged. "She kicked me out. Rented the place to a family from Red Bluff."

"Is that OK?"

"It's fine," he nodded. "I've moved in with Sunshine."

"Sunshine?"

"We've been seeing each other on and off for years. In San Anselmo."

"What about Villette?"

"Oh, Villette." He shrugged. "We're still friends, but Sunshine insists on monogamy. She's limited that way. I miss the, you know..."

The blow jobs, Jill thought.

"Anyway, I have a surprise." He handed Jill a printed postcard. "A small press in Berkeley is publishing my poems. Will you come to the book party?"

"That's great. Congratulations. I'd love to. Can I bring Margo?"

"Bring everybody you know," he laughed. "How's your novel about the schoolgirls?"

"I've got an agent."

"Way to go," he smiled.

"I ran into Dean today," Jill said to Margo as they walked along the Marina that evening.

"Dean?" Margo stopped.

"Dean of Dean and Vanessa, from my art class? Dean who was lovers with the drag queen?"

"Villette?"

"Yes, Villette. Good memory. He said Vanessa's living in the Caribbean on a sailboat with a sea captain. It sounds like she's pregnant."

"God help her," Margo said, crossing herself. "Did you ever call her?"

Jill shook her head. "I'm kind of afraid of her."

Margo nodded, taking Jill's hand as three women on roller blades skated past them at the Marina Green. "Do you think you're happier since you finished your novel and found an agent?" Margo pulled the dog out of the way of a new group of skaters.

"I think I'm happier because I realized how much I love you," Jill said, kissing Margo's cheek.

Margo laughed. "You've got all that energy in your pelvis now."

Jill nodded. "You do, too."

"How 'bout we drive to the Dock in Tiburon and watch the sunset?" Margo said, turning back toward Webster Street.

"Let's do," Jill said.

As they drove through Marin Headlands in the yellow Honda, Jill thought of Vanessa sailing in the Caribbean with a child inside her.

On the deck at the Dock, they ate cracked crab as the sun went down and sailboats slid into their slips.

"If you ever feel trapped again, you don't have to go searching for new friends," Margo said. "You know that." Jill looked quizzically at Margo, wondering where she was going with this. "I'll make love to you anytime you want. I'm not so uptight and distracted by things at work anymore. I feel a lot freer."

Jill laughed. "Maybe tonight?"

"You got it." Margo wrapped an arm around Jill, who gazed out at Angel Island remembering Vanessa, so sexy, so wasted, so willing to break the rules. Sometimes it took that, Jill knew, to learn what you love... and what you can't live without.

CARIBBEAN WAVE

Genevieve, my mother's best friend, has eyes the same blue as the Caribbean waves beneath the sloop's bow. In her bathing suit, her breasts are inches away as she passes me a plate of hummus and brie and Greek olives. We are running before the wind, upright and fast, our main sail swung out ninety degrees over the water, our jib split to the starboard side as we glide east down Sir Francis Drake Channel toward Virgin Gorda. Eddy, Genevieve's son, is at the helm. I remember him from childhood, much older than me, in his black leather jacket and motorcycle boots roaring up their driveway on his Triumph, a movie camera rolling. At the tiller now, he is tan and blond, his hair a little thinner, torso a little thicker, but he is still warm and upbeat and kind of crazy. He is telling me tales that are both funny and sad about his days as a helicopter pilot in Vietnam. My father is below, studying charts; my mother sunbathes on the foredeck. Genevieve's husband, red-faced, gripping a plastic cup of red wine, informs his son that the jib is luffing.

California and Vanessa and the winter rains seem far away as we pass Ginger Island on the starboard side. I am praying that it will happen, that Genevieve and I will be able to break from the group and

I may trace my fingertips across her cheek, along her neck, down her shoulder to her clavicle.

"How are you, Princess?" she asks me now, resting one hand on my knee. My birthday was the day we set sail, when she dubbed me "Princess" and continues to call me that. As I look into her eyes, she holds my gaze, laughing like a girl as she pushes a strand of white hair from her forehead. My stomach twirls. How much longer can I hang on to this edge?

I have lied. I want more than to touch Genevieve. Since we boarded in Road Town on Tortola, I have wanted to devour every part of her. In my dreams I see us on Virgin Gorda today, where we plan to hike and swim after lunch while my father and Genevieve's husband stay on board to organize the charts and galley, and Eddy, my mother, Genevieve, and I row to shore in the dinghy. Eddy and my mother are eager to go to the shops; he wants a new sun hat and a paperback novel to read in his bunk; she wants to buy more pineapple juice for piña coladas.

And that's just what happens. Mother and Eddy turn right for the shops, paying little attention to us as Mother tries to convince Eddy to make a documentary about the plight of unwed teenaged mothers, her latest cause. As they walk down the hill, Genevieve and I hike up a narrow trail that runs along the cliffs above the beach, a sudden breeze cooling us, the water below rocking our breath. I am sure she wants this as much as I do, but she will not make the first move. If we are to cross the chasm of age and propriety, I must initiate.

I can't recall exactly when this feeling started. I am thirty-five now; she is sixty. Perhaps it began when I was a child, blindfolded, at my cousin's birthday parties, when Genevieve touched my shoulders, turning me and the other children three times before we were allowed to slap the piñata with a plastic bat. On her visits to California, Eddy has sometimes hired me to give her massage if I'm not teaching. There has always been something about Genevieve, seductive and mysterious, despite her being entirely proper, that signals or triggers, I can't tell which, a sexual charge I don't feel with my mother's other friends. How my heart pounded in San Juan airport four days ago, where all of our planes converged, and she walked toward me, her straw hat cocked to one side, her blue cotton dress clinging to her hips, her smile so fond and sensual that I forgot my despair over Vanessa's most recent betrayal and my fatigue from the long flight from San Francisco.

We are ascending now, she in a sort of muumuu, me in shorts, my bikini underneath, ready to swim if we find the beach through this hot tangle of gorse. A lizard darts in front of her, and she cries out, reaching for my hand, which she continues to hold now as she asks about Vanessa.

"She sounds nutty," Genevieve says after I fill in some details.

"She is," I sigh. I'd left Margo to be with Vanessa, and Vanessa was driving me crazy.

"Not to change the subject..." Genevieve hesitates.

"Please do. It's over with Vanessa." I hope I'm right.

"When did you know?" She stops walking.

"Know?"

"That you..." She can't say it.

"That I'm a lesbian?"

"Am I out of line?" she blushes.

"I knew..." I choose my words carefully, which makes my speech odd and awkward, as if I had inhaled helium, as if each word were the kiss I long to place on her lips. "Maybe at my cousin's eighth birthday party," I say. "When you touched my shoulders and spun me around."

"Good heavens!" she cries primly. "You were a child!"

"I tried all my life not to love women," I inhale. "But I never really got the hang of men." I am afraid to break the spell by talking too much, but now that she has broached the subject, I want to pursue it without scaring her.

I ask how she spends her days. She says she loves her book club and must entertain her husband's business friends and spends much of her time trying to stop overpopulation.

"Overpopulation?"

"I screwed that up, didn't I?" she laughs. "Brought six children into the world, and now I'm telling everyone who'll listen to use birth control." Like my mother, like me, really, Genevieve supports many causes. My current cause is lobbying to have sex with her.

It is very hot. A green bird, perhaps a parrot, flies over us toward the ocean. "What do you read?" I ask.

"Say again?"

"In your book club?" We walk next to each other on the narrow path, arms linked. "Novels? Biographies? Liberation theology, like Mother?"

"Not liberation theology."

"In your book club?"

She thinks for a minute. "Anne Tyler spoke to us a few weeks ago. My friend Madelon brought her from Baltimore. Lovely woman. Very gifted and very odd. I think you'd like her."

"I loved *Dinner at the Homesick Restaurant.*"

"I'll ask Madelon to introduce you next time you come to town," she says. "She has wonderful insights about love, don't you think?"

I try to think what Anne Tyler's insights about love are. This may be the time to ask Genevieve *her* insights on love. "She's kind of a promoter of family values, don't you think? She's big on loyalty and family ties." I stop, distracted by the skirt of Genevieve's muumuu lifting in the breeze. Her legs are so smooth and sleek that I stumble. She catches me.

"I feel really hot," I gasp.

"Mad dogs and Irishmen," she laughs, leading me down a sandy path.

Englishmen, I correct in my mind.

The dunes open onto a white crescent beach, as graceful as a woman's body. At both ends of the cove, huge rocks drop into turquoise pools.

Miraculously, no boats are anchored here.

"How heavenly, my Princess."

There is an open, empty straw *palapa* halfway down the beach. I follow her to it. We spread our towels and lie down next to each other.

"What fun!" It is her Vassar 1940s voice. I am longing to hear something more real and urgent.

I inhale, asking the waves for courage, asking them what's next and begging them to forgive me for what I want to do. *This is your chance. Take it!* they say. I think of the witch Starhawk's precept I've heard her chant at ceremonies in California. *Every act of love and pleasure is a ritual in my name.*

"It's fun being together, alone, just the two of us? Don't you think?" I say.

She looks down at the handful of sand leaking through her long, tanned fingers. "Heavenly." Her body, her breasts are incredibly smooth and unwrinkled for someone sixty.

"You have the most beautiful body," I say.

She is blushing, but she leans against me and looks into my eyes. "So do you."

"I don't," I say quickly.

She takes my hand. "But you do, my darling. I know what I see." Now I am blushing. It is strange and exciting and weird to be this intimate with my mother's best friend. I lean back, letting one hand rest behind her right hip.

She sighs.

"Genevieve," I say, moving closer. "Do you believe in God?"

She laughs.

Before I can explain, she pulls me down on the sand beside her. Our lips touch and her hands wrap around me. We are pressed together, moving together. *Yes,* I think. *Yes.*

"I believe in God," she whispers as her knee presses between my legs, and her hands grasp my waist. "This is She, don't you think?"

I laugh, holding her head between my hands to find her lips. Her mouth opens and she brings my tongue into her mouth.

"I've never done this," she whispers.

I can't answer. Desire has wadded my mouth with cotton. Her lips are turning me molten; my breath catches. Her legs open as I draw down her bathing suit, and her fingers slip under my bikini bottoms. "I want to, but I'm afraid," she says.

"I love you," I whisper.

"Do you? Aren't I so old?"

"You are perfect." The waves come closer as her fingers brush my clit.

She pulls my lips to hers again, then leans back, looking into my eyes. "I thought I'd invited you on this sail for Eddy, but I wanted you for me." I cannot believe the heat those words raise in my legs. I want to swallow her, devour her, feel her body go down through my throat, into my breath, my stomach and my womb. I look into her eyes; her gaze is hot, surprised, and eager and makes my clit stand up and my insides turn over and tumble in a long hot explosion of lust and expectation. "Genevieve," I cry.

Her arms tighten around me. "I'm yours," she whispers.

My lips move from her salty ones down and down until I am licking her hard on, devouring her, feeling the arc of heaven swirl inside her, as it has, as it does, inside me. This woman has found my broken garden, loved my scattered sandbox, is spinning me back and carrying me forward. She will not let go of me, ever; I know that. She will not let me fail, or fall. I know it by her embrace, by her cry of excitement as she contracts around my fingers. I am coming and crying. She is coming, too.

"I want those years back," she whispers. "When I didn't know."

"You knew," I say, kissing her neck, her eyes, her hair as she arches again and rises and shouts, so generous, so responsive, so hot and kind that I am coming again, holding her closer than Vanessa or Margo would ever allow.

The air is softer but still hot. We are naked and alone and sandy and wrapped in each other's arms, dripping in sweat and salt, serenaded by the waves, rejoicing in our incredible, ecstatic accomplishment. We walk naked into the aquamarine water, my body white and long; hers, full and tan, breasts and hips streaked with sand. I swim into her arms, wrapping my legs around her waist in the deeper water. She rocks me against her, holding me tight as the current laps over us. "This is heaven," she laughs. "Absolute heaven." Her white hair turns gold in the sun. "I have never been so happy."

"Tell me," I say.

"I love this more than anything, ever."

"Really?" A frigate bird squawks above us. "Will you come to California?"

"Yes, my darling." She gazes at the horizon, where a sail catches the sky. "I have two sons there, and now I have you."

"We should go back." I unwrap myself from her body.

"I wonder what they'll think." She kisses my cheek, then her eyes meet mine solemnly. "This is a great, huge love," she says, wiping something from her eye. "You understand that?"

"Huge," I say. "And forbidden."

"Don't say that." Her face looks suddenly tight and sad.

"But it is."

"I want you again," she whispers as we pull on our swimsuits in the palapa. She brushes her hand through my hair so tenderly, in such a familiar way that my heart trips. But we don't have time. Arm in arm, we climb the path to the wider trail, then look behind us at the blue cove where we lay, then ahead of us, down at the dock by the shops. There are my mother and Eddy, waiting for us, still laughing and talking. I wrap my arm around her waist; she wraps an arm around mine.

"Where have you two been?" My mother gives us an odd once-over, eyebrows raised.

"We went for a delicious swim," Genevieve says. "Have you had fun shopping?"

"Fabulous," Eddy says, showing off his new white seafarer's brimmed hat. My mother laughs. For a moment, she looks so happy I wonder if she and Eddy... But no, that couldn't be.

Eddy rows the dinghy back to the boat, where we have cocktails and dinner. Genevieve and I glance at each other across the cockpit. Much later, when Genevieve's husband has gone to bed in the forward cabin, and my parents are asleep below, Eddy and Genevieve and I sit beneath the stars, he smoking a joint, me drinking a beer, and she sipping a bourbon highball.

"I'm loving this," Genevieve says. "Can we stay forever?"

Her son grins, his smile bright in the moonlight. "Sign me up."

Genevieve puts an arm around my waist, looking at me with such longing I ache for her all over again. "What about you, my Princess?"

"Absolutely," I say, falling into her blue, blue eyes. "Count me in."

ROUGH CROSSING

On the New York State Thruway, the trees, naked in the snow, remind Jill of what she and her father are trying to forget: The thin bones, the frightened eyes, the frozen hillside where they buried her mother four days ago, on the coldest day since 1913, which just happens to be the year her mother was born.

It's gray from here to Canada, Jill thinks, tuning the dial to WABC, the only station her father's Dodge Dart can pick up. To the north and west, the Catskill Mountains rise abruptly; to the east stretch the sturdy hills of the Hudson River Valley. Jill glances over to see if Stevie Wonder's "Isn't She Lovely?" is bothering her father. Nope. He's fallen asleep, newspaper in hand, reading glasses perched on his nose, Irish tweed cap on his head.

"I'm a mess," her mother said last week in Philadelphia, staring hopelessly at the plastic bag into which her poop flowed. That day Jill had been bathing her with a warm washrag, holding her breath as she wiped the skin near the purple stoma, the part of her mother's gut that popped out through her abdomen and connected to her colostomy bag.

"You're heavenly good to me," her mother said, her gray-blue eyes reaching for Jill as Jill patted her down with a towel, then rubbed Keri lotion from the hospital over her mother's dry arms and legs.

"I love you, Mom." Jill kissed her cool, swollen knuckles. "I'm sorry you feel so rotten."

Stop thinking about it, Jill tells herself. *You did what you could. Think of Pip. Think of Margo and Ellen. In an hour, you'll be with them, and you can relax.*

"You and your father need to get away," Margo had said at the funeral last week in Baltimore. She and Ellen had driven half the night to get there. "Come stay with us in Hudson."

"Won't we be in the way?" Jill glanced at Ellen, who could be moody and brusque when friends came to stay.

"We wouldn't ask you if we didn't want you," Ellen said, touching Jill's hand. "You both need a break."

Jill felt more comfortable with Margo than any person in the world. Around Margo, she could be sad and pale and insecure. Her eyes could be swollen, her hair ragged, her heart a wreck, and Margo would still love her, laugh at her jokes, make the coffee twice as strong as she and Ellen drank it simply because that's how Jill liked it. Ellen was more challenging. She could turn nasty in an instant, explode without warning, then pour on the charm an hour later. Jill tried to keep her visits with Margo short to avoid Ellen's meltdowns. But this time, Jill was prepared to risk an attack because she and her father both desperately needed to escape the house in Philadelphia, now so empty and sad after her mother's pills and creams were put away and the medical supply company had taken back the oxygen compressor and portable toilet. And her mother was gone.

Jill's father had agreed to the trip immediately. Like Jill, he felt safe with Margo, who seemed a stand-in, in a way, for his missing daughter, Jill's older sister, Meg, who'd refused to visit her mother when she was dying and did not show up for her funeral. Margo had been kind to Jill's father for nearly a decade, since that day that seemed so long ago when Jill and Margo had taken Amtrak from New York to tell Jill's parents that they were lovers, lesbians, in a committed relationship. Even after they'd moved to California, and Jill had fallen for Vanessa and broken up with Margo, Margo had kept in touch with Jill's parents and helped Jill move out of Vanessa's house that New Year's Eve when Vanessa had left again for the Caribbean. "Margo is," her mother had said more than once, "by far the most decent, kindest *friend* you've ever had. It's too bad you let her go."

"I haven't let her go," Jill would say. "She's my best friend."

Margo had gotten together with Ellen in San Francisco, soon after Jill had moved out to be with Vanessa. As Jill and Vanessa crashed and burned, Margo and Ellen thrived, moving back East after a few years to the Hudson River Valley to be closer to Margo's family, to freelance jobs and to a small town where they could afford to buy a house. Jill missed Margo terribly when she'd left California because Margo was her best friend.

Now here Margo is, waving from the front porch of their white clapboard house as Jill and her father pull into their driveway. The house, a few blocks from the Hudson River, has a matching white barn and garage in the back, and a yard where the cat and the dachshunds play. The cat is now curled on the radiator in the kitchen, and the dogs yelp and leap as Jill and her father carry in their suitcases. The warmth of the house, the cozy familiarity, make Jill cry.

Margo cooks sole wrapped in asparagus, a recipe Jill and Margo discovered in the *New York Times Large Type Cookbook* when they had lived together in San Francisco and were learning to cook. They eat now at the same oak dining room table that Jill and Margo bought on Fourteenth Street in Oakland when they first arrived in San Francisco. Margo kept it in the divorce, since Jill had no place to put it in the small studio she'd rented on Filbert Street.

As they eat ice cream sandwiches for dessert, Margo mentions the famous heavyweight boxing champ who trains at a gym in their town. Margo and Ellen sometimes see the boxer, an odd, lonely figure driving down Main Street in his blue Rolls Royce, stopping to shake hands with the teenagers who ogle his car. His trainer has recently died, and the boxer is bereft. Until her mother's death, Jill had not noticed how frequently death works its way into conversations.

Jill's father, usually chatty and expansive after two cocktails and a glass of wine, says little and goes to bed right after they eat, exhausted from months of caring for Jill's mother. Jill and Margo and Ellen sit by the fire in the living room. Jill can hear his feet thudding across the floor above them. He is unpacking his pajamas and shaving kit, his woolen socks and new book on trout fishing that his friend Fred gave him for Christmas.

Margo, who knows Jill is always cold, places a quilt over her and hands her a dachshund to hold as a log pops in the fireplace.

"I met someone," Jill says, finally relaxing.

"Who? Where?" Ellen sits up, eyes bright.

"In Philadelphia."

"You're a fast operator," Margo laughs. "Tell us about her."

Jill closes her eyes, thinking of Pip.

Pip is petite and funny and lives in the same apartment building as Solomon, Jill's best friend in Philadelphia. Everything Pip owns is tiny. Her apartment, her feet, her pug dogs, even the pony bottles of Rolling Rock beer she drinks as she chain-smokes. Pip's father committed suicide when she was twelve. She is a bookkeeper for an arts organization in the day; at night, she sometimes teaches ballroom dancing at Arthur Murray Dance Studio.

Last week, the night before Jill's mother died, Jill and Solomon and Pip and Marcia, Pip's lover, planned to go dancing at Sneaker's, a woman's bar on Second Street. Solomon thought it would be therapeutic for Jill to get out of the house and have some fun. Jill wasn't so sure, but at eight, she drove her parents' car to Pip's to pick them up. It was very cold. Pip wore a miniskirt and tiny red shoes and a petite red jacket. Marcia and Solomon weren't there. At the last minute, Solomon had to take his friend Ernesto to the hospital because of a fever.

"Where's Marcia?" Jill asked.

"She's too tired," Pip said. "She's on her feet all day working at her parents' dry cleaners. Says the air at Sneaker's is too nasty and smoky."

"Worse than a dry cleaner's?"

Solomon has told Jill that Marcia, who has a seven-year-old daughter named Rebecca, is often too tired to go out at night and is somewhat possessive. Jill doesn't miss Marcia, but she wishes Solomon were with them because she hardly knows Pip. Upstairs, at the bar, Pip orders a Rolling Rock, and Jill, who stopped drinking after her first break-up with Vanessa, sips a ginger ale. When they go downstairs, Jill feels way too sober to dance. "Marcia was right," she shouts over the music.

Pip raises her eyebrows. "About what?"

"The smoke here is bad."

Pip lights a cigarette. Standing against the mirrored wall, they stare at the bodies moving under the strobe lights. Jill is nervous, afraid Pip will make her dance.

"Let's dance," Pip says, pulling Jill toward the dance floor.

"I'm a terrible dancer."

"I bet you're not." Pip pulls her into the mass of bodies and blinking strobe lights.

Jill feels like the Tin Woodman, with every joint stiff and thirsty for oil. Pip vogues and moonwalks and moves so expertly that many of the bar-goers stop to watch her. Jill starts to think about going home. But the music slows, and Pip places Jill's hands on her waist, moving so close Jill can feel a jolt of hot pink neon in her legs.

"Wow." She has not felt anything like that in months. Or is it years?

Gladys Knight, steamy and urgent, is singing "You're the Best Thing That Ever Happened to Me." Pip smiles. "I'll lead."

Jill can feel Pip's fingers moving down the small of her back, stopping at Jill's butt, then pulling Jill closer. She can feel Pip against her and taste the sweat in her baby-blond hair, which is as drenched as if she'd been swimming. "You feel nice," Jill says. Lust has reduced her to monosyllables.

Pip looks up. "Are you OK?"

"Good," Jill swallows. Pip's breath on the side of her neck makes her shiver. "Today's been..."

"Don't explain."

"My mother had a really bad day." Jill fights tears. She won't have a mother much longer.

Pip nods, resting her cheek against Jill's shoulder. "I like you a lot, you know."

"I like you, too." Jill feels agonizingly sober. There is cotton in her mouth and a vice tightening around her neck. She hasn't touched a woman since forever. But Pip's legs, coaxing her closer, are changing that.

When the music changes, Pip stands on her tiptoes and kisses Jill on the lips. The friendly liking of Pip suddenly turns into irresistible magnets. When Jill closes her eyes, colors shout: Purples and reds and electronic greens follow a navy-blue ocean at night, when the swells break and foam dollops the sand.

Pip is all sinew and motion, and Jill is miraculously following, led by the rhythm in Pip's hips. Pip is sculpting her, letting Jill sculpt her right back, the music sucking them deeper into each other. Jill remembers something like this once, in California, with Vanessa. But that was different because she and Vanessa had snorted cocaine. Jill is clean and sober now but is somehow able to dance.

They move to an empty table in a dark corner. Pip drops onto Jill's lap. The attraction is pulling Jill's heart down through her chest and into her legs. Pip moans; Jill feels heaven moving in her thighs.

"Did we dance or did we... make love?" Jill asks, driving back to Pip's at Tenth and Pine.

Pip laughs. "I'm not sure."

"Marry me," Jill says double parking on Tenth Street. "Come live with me in California."

Pip sits up, her eyes solemn. "I'm with Marcia, you know."

That does not explain anything to Jill, certainly not the pulsing in her body and the neon of Pip's touch. She wonders momentarily if Pip loves Marcia as much as she thinks she does. Pip's hand touches Jill's knee. "Why don't you come up?"

"What about Marcia?" Jill says, looking for a parking space.

"She's at her place. She went to bed hours ago. She won't call."

Jill follows Pip into her apartment, which is one floor above Solomon's. Pip turns on a small electric heater, makes Jill a glass of peppermint tea, opens a tiny beer for herself, and lights a cigarette. She sits next to Jill on the sofa, stroking both of her pugs.

"So?" Jill smiles. "What are we going to do?"

"Let's lie down." Pip points to her loft bed, carrying Jill's glass of tea up the wooden ladder. They strip in the darkness.

Jill feels like her heart might stop as she presses against the smooth length of Pip's perfect body. They are dancing again, Pip sliding over Jill, under her, around her, everywhere.

"I'm not scared of you anymore," Pip whispers.

Jill catches her breath. "Scared of me?"

"I'm too turned on to be *really* scared."

"Why scared?" Jill asks, barely able to talk.

"Because you're tall. And sarcastic. And you never noticed me at Solomon's before."

"I *did* notice you."

"You know what I mean. I noticed *you* two years ago when Solomon introduced us. But you didn't pay the slightest attention to me."

"I was obsessed with Vanessa. And you were with Lisa."

"Lisa and I had broken up when Solomon introduced us."

"Seemed like you were still with her. You did everything together."

"I liked you, though." Pip's thighs grip Jill's. Wet and slippery, Pip drags herself against Jill, moaning softly.

"We're like O'Henry's 'Gift of the Magi,'" Jill says.

Pip laughs. "When I was free, you were married. Now I'm married, and you're free."

"I cut my hair; you give me a barrette."

Pip dances on top of Jill. "I'm in love with your whole fucking body," she says, her hands on Jill's hips as she presses herself hard and rhythmically along Jill's leg. Jill moans as Pip goes down, down, down on her, across and back, across and back with her tongue in a smooth, elastic moonwalk. Jill is coming and crying, pulling Pip close to her, tighter and tighter so she can't lose her.

"Fuck me," Pip says, arching and crying and pulling Jill into her, wet and coming all over. "I love you."

When dawn edges through the gray curtains, and Pip's dogs bark for their breakfast, Jill drives home and tiptoes past her parent's bedroom. They do not know that she's been gone all night. Later, Jill's mother, without her wig, head bald, leans helplessly back against the mahogany headboard, mouth wide and gasping for air. A new red rash, some kind of different cancer, Jill's father thinks, covers her arms and breasts. All morning, the mucus rumbles in her lungs, and Jill understands why this sound is called the death rattle. It is like no ordinary cough. It is a low, frightening cauldron of phlegm that bubbles and chokes off the air. Jill sits next to her on the bed holding her mother's bony hand. *Memorize those eyes,* Jill thinks to herself, remembering a song written by a friend in California. She will not have a mother much longer.

The phone rings in her mother's bedroom. Jill hopes it is Pip. But it is her mother's best friend, Genevieve, in Washington, D.C.

"How is she?" Genevieve says. "How are *you,* my Princess?"

"She's not that great today," Jill says, staring at her mother's bald head. "I miss you."

"There's a train to Philadelphia at noon. I'd can be there by teatime."

"Um..." Jill looks at her mother, covering the mouthpiece with her hand. "Genevieve can visit today, Mom. There's a train at—"

"No," her mother whispers, barely opening her eyes. "No visitors. Only if Meg..."

"Sure. OK." Jill's sister Meg will not be calling, Jill is certain. For one thing, she does not have a telephone. For another, she despises her family.

"Mother's not up to it," Jill tells Genevieve, who knows this is very bad news because Jill's mother is a self-described "people person."

"She's not... she doesn't feel too good." Jill can hear Genevieve crying. "But she loves you. I love you."

"I love you, too, Princess," Genevieve gulps. "Call me anytime. Night or day. You know. If anything... changes."

"Jill," her mother whispers at six o'clock that night. "You're holding my hand too tight."

"Wow. Sorry, Ma." Jill releases her grip on her mother's fingers, fighting her tears. At 8 P.M., her mother's breathing almost disappears between those terrifying rattles. Jill watches her chest; her father watches her chest, keeping his fingers on her wrist, feeling her pulse, which he says is very rapid. For months, he has bathed her, helped her to the toilet, changed and cleaned her plastic stomach bag, offered her sips of water, spooned her ice cream when she refused her trays of food. He is losing his wife of forty-two years.

"I love you, Mom," Jill says. "Genevieve loves you. Dad loves you. Aunt Jill and Uncle Bruce love you. So many people love you. They're all right here with you, with us, right now."

"Meg called?" Her mother's voice is a tiny scratch of sound.

Jill shakes her head. "Meg doesn't have a phone." When Meg had a phone, she hung up on her mother and her father and Jill.

At eight p.m., her mother gasps for air and goes quiet.

Jill's father looks at his watch. "She was a remarkable woman. I hope her life will be a model to us all."

Jill does not take her eyes from her mother's chest. "Is she...?"

He nods, looking at his watch. "At 8:02 P.M."

Her mother's hand is still warm. Jill looks up at the ceiling. She has heard on TV shows and read in books that dead people sometimes linger in the room, watching their loved ones from above, from the ceiling. "I love you, Mom," Jill says, looking up at the wall of family photos her mother has been looking at for month. "I'm here with you, Mom. We love you so much. Everyone loves you. Don't be scared." Jill herself is very scared. Scared of not having a mother. Scared she might crack up.

In his study across from the bedroom, Jill's father is calling the funeral home, giving them the address, then calling her mother's oncologist, requesting an autopsy so that her father can be sure that her colon was the primary source of this nightmare cancer. He calls Genevieve. "We lost her tonight, at 8:02 P.M." He calls Aunt Jill and Uncle Bruce. His voice is metallic. A stab of pain cuts through Jill's chest. It must be true. Her mother's life is over. Her father is announcing her death. Jill stays in the room with her mother, watching the undertakers slide her into a black bag, zip her up and carry her down the steps on a gurney. Then they slip her into the hearse like they are gliding a pizza into an oven. *This is what it is like,* Jill thinks, *when your mother dies. Telephone calls are made, and strangers take her away in a bag.*

Jill sleeps in Ellen's office, upstairs, next to the guest room, where her father is sleeping. Ellen has painted her room a deep dark green with white-trimmed windows. By her writing desk an ancient, furless teddy bear sits on an antique wooden sled. On the windowsill Jill is surprised to see a black-and-white photo of Ellen as a child wearing a Saint Louis Cardinals baseball cap. Jill was born in Saint Louis although she has no memory of the place. Ellen was born in Detroit.

In the morning, Margo and Ellen make a fire in the living room, make Jill and her father breakfast, serve hot chocolate and grilled cheese sandwiches for lunch. Her father is getting laryngitis and goes to bed right after dinner.

"Tell us more about Pip," Margo says.

Jill leans back, her stomach swirling as she thinks about her. "She is tiny and funny and surprising."

"Is she free?" Margo says, knowing Jill's bad track record. "Or is she with someone?"

Busted, Jill thinks. *Margo knows me too well.* "She's with someone called Marcia."

Margo sighs.

Ellen studies Jill. "Just a diversion, right? Something to distract you from your mother."

Jill swallows. Her night with Pip had certainly been distracting. But it feels like more.

"It's lust," Margo says, sipping her tea. "You barely know her."

"You don't know that, Margo," says Ellen, who has always loved a good fight.

Margo shakes her head, leaning back in her chair. "I *do* know that. You don't know Pip, do you Jill?"

Jill feels stupid. She should not have told them. "Pip says she loves Marcia, but she was very friendly in bed." Jill is getting excited thinking about Pip. "She seems to really like me. And I like her."

"Of course, she likes you, Jill. You're very likable. But lust isn't love," Margo sighs. "I just wish you'd find someone who's available."

"Maybe she'll become available, Margo," Ellen says. "You don't know."

"She lives in Philadelphia, Ellen. Jill lives in California."

Jill knows Margo is thinking of Vanessa, who was never free, sometimes with Dean, sometimes with his sister, sometimes with a sailor, sometimes with strangers, all while claiming to love Jill more than any of them.

"Ellen wasn't available when you two got together," Jill says, trying to defend herself.

"Hardly the same," Margo huffs, face reddening.

"She's right," Ellen grins. "I was still with Rosa."

"Your break-up with her was long overdue," Margo says. "You were practically free."

"Is anyone free?" Jill whispers. She is falling asleep in front of the fire, dreaming of Pip.

Margo and Ellen drive Jill and her father up into the mountains, to a fork where seven raging creeks meet. It is too cold for her father to fish or even to walk beyond the car. They eat brown trout, baked potatoes, and Caesar salad at a hunting lodge with deer and elk and bear heads hanging from the walls. Jill's father clears his throat as he scoops his butterscotch sundae.

"Two years ago, after my wife's biopsy, when we knew the node on her neck was malignant, but we didn't know the primary source, she suggested we sail across the Atlantic, from the Canary Islands to Bermuda, on a Merriweather Post schooner called *Flying Cloud*. She cashed out a CD and made the reservations, and we had a fine time until the ship got caught in a storm that blew out several of the sails, forcing us to motor the final three days of the trip. A lot of the passengers were seasick, but my wife was a great sport. Didn't mind the rough crossing, never complained and kept everyone laughing."

"She was a good woman," Margo says.

Jill's father removes a clean white handkerchief from his pocket and blows his nose.

Back in the car, his laryngitis is worse.

For four nights they stay in the warm house with Margo and Ellen and the dogs and cat. On the last night, when Jill and her father have gone to bed, Ellen and Margo argue loudly in the kitchen. Jill can hear Ellen yell her name but can't make out the words. She calls Pip from the phone in Ellen's office. Her hands shake when hears Pip's voice.

"I can't stop thinking about you," Pip says.

"Ellen is screaming at Margo in the kitchen," Jill whispers.

Pip laughs. "Couples fight, you know."

"Do you and Marcia fight?"

"She wasn't too happy when I told her you spent the night."

"You told her?" Jill holds her breath.

"Most of it."

Did you tell her you love me?

"Call me the minute you get home."

In the morning, Margo and Ellen say nothing about their fight and make tuna fish sandwiches and chocolate chip cookies for Jill and her father's drive home. They all try to be cheerful. "I can't thank you enough," Jill's father says, embracing both women.

"Come back," Margo says. "Anytime."

"I've joined a trout fishing club in the Poconos. I hope you'll come fish with me in the summer."

"We'd love to," Margo says.

"Let us know what happens with Pip," Ellen whispers.

"I will," Jill says, embracing them both, grateful for the warmth of their welcome.

Jill's father suggests they drive back via Ocean City, New Jersey. It is a much longer way, but Jill's mother loved the sea, and they both somehow hope that she might communicate with them at the ocean. But the day is so cold they can only walk briefly on the beach, and no spirit visitations occur. The sky is blue and the waves hard, immense and relentless. Jill tosses a couple smooth stones into the water, inhaling the roar and roll and grind of the surf. She and her father eat the sandwiches from Margo and Jill in the parking lot by the ocean.

"Did you hear Ellen and Margo fight last night?" Jill asks her father.

"Did they fight?"

"You didn't hear them yelling?"

Jill's father eats his cookie and follows a cormorant with his binoculars. "Slept very well. Sorry you heard them fighting. They were very nice to have us."

"Very," Jill says. Her father's hearing is getting worse.

It is too late to call Pip when they get home. The next day Jill tries to reach Pip after she and her father take twenty-two bags of her mother's clothes — blouses, evening gowns, costume jewelry, shorts, slacks and sweaters — to the hospital thrift store, around the corner from Pip's apartment. The store manager tells Jill she has overestimated the financial value of her mother's possessions and will not give her a receipt for the amount Jill thinks they are worth. Jill cries as she and her father leave the store. She reaches Solomon from a pay phone. "We just took Mother's things to the thrift shop, and we're afraid to go home. It's too sad."

"Come for tea." Solomon is exhausted from taking Ernesto back to the hospital. He is losing Ernesto to an opportunistic disease.

When her father uses the bathroom, Solomon says, "Pip told me about your... night on the town." Jill feels her legs go soft. "She's committed to Marcia, you know."

Jill nods. "Yes."

"But she really likes you."

"I really like her."

Pip comes over the next night, after dinner. Jill wants to take her upstairs to bed, but her father stays up late with them telling Pip in his hoarse voice about the nice women in New York State whom they visited. "They're wonderful girls, Margo and Ellen. Margo was Jill's..." He hesitates, looking at Jill.

"My lover," Jill finishes.

"Lucky Margo," Pip says, touching Jill's hand. At ten o'clock, Jill drives Pip home.

"Can I come up?" Jill asks, desperate to hold Pip. "Is Marcia..."

"She's at her place. Come in."

Inside, Jill plays with the dogs while Pip opens a beer. Jill lays her head in Pip's lap and kisses her fingers, which are very cold. "Can we curl up in your loft? I'll warm you up."

"I'm with Marcia, you know."

"You keep telling me."

"Because it's true."

Jill sighs. "So where are we?"

"I'm... not free."

"Were you free the night we went dancing?"

Pip chews her lip.

"Were you?"

Pip inhales. "You knew about Marcia. I never lied."

Jill sighs. "What did you tell her?"

Pip sips her beer. "I told her I was attracted to you."

"And?"

"That you stayed over." Pip's voice is tired and tense. There are shadows under her eyes. Her face looks older, not like a child's, the way it does sometimes, but a middle-aged woman's. Her shoulders are slightly stooped, her skin ashen from too many cigarettes, her jowls swollen from beer. "She told me I can do whatever I want." Pip's hands shake as she lights another cigarette.

"Don't smoke that." Jill crushes the cigarette in the ashtray.

"She says I can do whatever I want, but if I go to bed with you, we're over." Pip stares at the ashtray.

"So?" Jill waits.

"I can hold you like this," Pip says. "With your head in my lap."

Jill doesn't understand. "What?"

"That's all I can do."

"Have you taken it back?" Jill asks.

"Taken what back?"

"That you really, really like me."

"I do really like you." She lights a cigarette. Jill doesn't stop her this time although the smoke surrounds her. "But I'm committed to Marcia." Pip says it stoically, like a soldier packing for the front. She moves Jill's head gently, opens another beer and sits down, easing Jill's head back onto her lap. Jill feels the neon jolting in her legs, but she also feels angry. She has no right to be angry. She knows that. It's her own fault. Pip is not free.

"So, we can't sleep together again?" Jill presses. "But I can put my head in your lap?"

Pip stares at the fire escape that goes past the kitchen window. "More or less. As long as... things don't escalate."

"Like the Vietnam War?"

"Not funny." Pip bites her lip.

"Do you know how turned on I am lying with my head in your lap?" Jill says, feeling wet and sticky in her legs.

"I do," Pip says.

"Because you're turned on, too?"

Pip takes a long drag of her cigarette. "Yes."

"You want to, don't you?"

"But I can't."

Jill pushes Pip's hand away and stands up, tears leaking from her eyes. Pip offers her a Kleenex. When the phone rings, they both jump, afraid it's Marcia. But it's Jill's father, asking her to come home.

Jill, so turned on she could scream, takes a breath. Her mother is dead, and her father wants her to come home, and Pip is committed to Marcia.

"Are you angry?" Pip says at the door.

"Angry and horny."

"I'm sorry," Pip says.

At home, her father's bedroom light is on but he has fallen asleep, a book in his hands. He is lying on the far side, where he always sleeps, leaving the near side of the bed for his wife.

A year and a half later, on a visit to Philadelphia, Jill notices that her father still sleeps on the far side, close to the edge of the bed, leaving room for Jill's mother. On that same visit, she and her father, both feeling low, have an idea. They pack the car and drive to New York State to see Margo and Ellen. Because it is summer, the trees on the New York State Thruway are green and lush, beckoning them north, completely different from that cold March after her mother's death when the trees were bare and gray and the ground was frozen. Margo and Ellen are waiting on the front porch, suntanned and smiling. After Jill's father goes to bed, they stretch out in the living room with the dogs and the cat.

"Have you seen Pip?" Ellen asks, a red dachshund curled by her side.

Jill feels a tear and a shiver of neon at the mention of Pip's name. "She moved to Hawaii. The Big Island. Near Volcano."

Margo's blue eyes widen. "Did her lover go with her? Marcia, was it?"

"Yes, Marcia," Jill sighs.

Margo squints at Jill. "You still have a thing for Pip?"

Jill looks from Ellen to Margo, who is waiting for her answer.

"You do, don't you?"

"I do," Jill says.

"You should visit her," Ellen says.

Margo frowns. "You wouldn't consider moving to Hawaii, would you? Isn't California far enough away? We'd never see you."

Ellen grins. "Maybe you *should* move to satisfy your lust."

"Lust, for sure. Not love." Margo strokes the doxie's ears.

"It *was* love." Jill looks up at the many shelves of books around the room, a few written by Ellen, a few by Jill, a few by Deena and Lana and several of their other friends. "I flew out there, you know."

Margo sits up. "What?" The dog glances at her nervously.

Jill is thinking of the blue ocean, the smell of plumeria, the thrill of

Pip's body, all hers for two weeks. "She asked me to come live with her."

"I hope you're not considering it." Margo shakes her head.

"I *did* consider it." Jill swallows.

"What changed?" Ellen leans forward. The dog next to her jumps down and trots over to Margo, who picks him up.

"You were going to move?" Margo stares at her.

"I was, until Pip's neighbor found her lying on the kitchen floor."

"Oh, no." Margo shakes her head. "Why? What happened?"

"Is she OK?" Ellen sits up.

"Pretty much," Jill shrugs. "She's working again."

"Wow," Ellen says.

Jill inhales. "Marcia flew out with her daughter to take care of her and decided to stay." Jill can feel tears welling in her chest. "They bought a house together."

Margo rises and sits next to Jill. "I'm sorry, sweetheart." She puts an arm around Jill, who wipes away tears.

"So she left her parents' dry-cleaning business?" Ellen is fascinated.

"Yep. They got married, and Solomon gave Pip away."

"Did you go?" Ellen's eyes are wide.

"I thought about it."

"Jesus, Mary, and Joseph." Margo flips on the overhead fan to cool down the room. "She wasn't free, Jill. She never was."

Jill can feel the neon racing in her knees. "Dad even considered moving there with me. Before Pip's stroke."

"I can't believe you didn't tell us." Margo shakes her head.

"Has she stopped drinking?" Ellen's eyes are bright. She is loving this dyke drama.

Jill rubs her eyes wondering if the cat is making them itch. "She gave up everything. Alcohol, cigarettes, beer, and pot."

"Everything but Marcia," Ellen says.

Jill nods. Upstairs, in this house, she hears her father's footsteps on the floor as he prepares to slide into the far side of the bed, leaving plenty of room for her mother.

"Let's never get sick," Margo says, glancing at Ellen.

"Never," Jill says.

"Ever," Ellen says.

"And let's never get sex and love confused," Margo says, looking at Jill.

"Her mother was dying, Margo," Ellen says. "Anyway, everyone gets sex and love confused, especially in the beginning, when you don't know if it's lust or something else. You and I didn't know."

"I did," Margo says. She looks at Jill. "You'll find both one of these days, Jill."

"Hope so," Jill says, grateful that the neon pinks of Pip and their electric bursts of pleasure had made the rough crossing nearly bearable.

IN ANOTHER COUNTRY

We are three women who speak no Spanish, Jill thinks, as she follows her cousin Elizabeth, and Sylvie, the landscape designer, through the aisles of a nursery in Puerto Vallarta. It is the third nursery they have visited this morning because they are selecting plants for Elizabeth's *casa,* pulling them out of their neat rows and into the muddy aisles. Sylvie, petite, suntanned, and strong, with a stomach that is gloriously flat, is in constant motion, a hummingbird in red visor, red-striped shirt, red shorts, and red Crocs, studying the ginger and vinca and yucca, calling the plants by their Latin names, making notes on her clipboard, turning back to seek the others' opinion. Her dark, quick eyes spot the finest plants in seconds. Jill herself is tall and pale. She does not, at this moment, mind the tropical heat that reddens her face beneath her straw hat, or the mud, which sucks over her flip-flops, soiling the cuffs of her white pants. She has escaped American Thanksgiving and is grateful for that. She has no family besides Elizabeth. And she thinks she may be falling in love with Sylvie. It is high time she stopped seeing Vanessa, with her on-and-off husband, and her on-and-off girl-friends, and her adorable daughter.

Elizabeth is fingering her yellow-gold necklace, her brown eyes focused on the plants as well as a deeper problem — *her husband,* Jill guesses — who seems perpetually distracted by his businesses, his houses, his sports cars, his motorcycles, and his greenbelt projects near San Francisco. He is always building or remodeling something — a ranch in Sonoma, a mansion in Pacific Heights, a villa in Tuscany, and now, he has ordered a new garden at their *casa* in Puerto Vallarta. The sunlight catches the links of Elizabeth's gold necklace, dazzling in this earthy outpost on the edge of town, with its smell of diesel fuel, sewage, and *tortillas*.

Turning, Elizabeth speaks to Jorge, her chauffeur, who trails behind them at a respectable distance, his masculine pride long ago chastened by the rich *señora* and the American guests who often stay at the house. "This would work at the *casa*, don't you think, Jorge?" she asks. "Shall we get *cuatro, cinco* maybe?"

"*Claro, señora. Cinco.*" He nods to the nursery owner, jingling the car keys in his pocket. Jill wonders if Jorge thinks *he* should be selecting the plants, since, he, after all, lives at the *casa* and will water them each day when the *señora* and her husband are back in San Francisco, which is most of the time.

The manager's office, where Elizabeth is attempting to pay her bill, is outside beneath an umbrella at a worn oak desk in the dirt and flanked by two plastic lawn chairs and a cluster of dusty palms. The transaction is long and slow, all by hand at this outpost, where there seem to be no computers or *calculadoras*. The rotund, sullen *señora* who runs the nursery writes everything by hand, pausing, sighing, sending the *braceros* back to the aisles again and again to check prices, count and recount the *dropsidea* and ferns, *palmas* and *hierbas de plumas* the *señoras* have selected.

Jill gazes across the road as school children descend from an ancient blue and white transit bus that is no doubt a cast-off from a school district in Southern California. By the slough, one of the children enters a tiny adobe house with an aluminum roof that is lopsided and dented in the middle.

"I've got to have a Coke," Elizabeth says when they are back in the white Datsun, headed toward town and the *casa*. Although he does not appear to have heard, Jorge screeches to a halt in front of a crumbling grocery store, where bananas are spoiling on the counter and some cartons of Kellogg's Corn Flakes are collecting dust. Elizabeth is so thrilled by the sight of the huge red cooler full of Coca-Colas that she does not care that the proprietor is overcharging them by hundreds of pesos.

Cokes now in hand, Jill sits in front with Jorge while Elizabeth and Sylvie sit in back, reviewing the garden project and what plants will go where. The car bumps and rattles south, past the airport, through the stone streets of Puerto Vallarta and on to the road south along the cliffs. Because Sylvie has found all the plants she needs for the *casa*, she and Elizabeth decide they will not have to fly to Guadalajara to visit more nurseries tomorrow. They laugh with relief and recall the high-lights of this morning — the intense heat, the endless aisles of tropical plants, their terrible Spanish, and the unpleasant *señora* who seemed to give them the *mal de ojo*, the evil eye, as she wrote and rewrote the bill on the crooked oak table.

We are all forty-three years *old,* Jill thinks. *Thirty years ago at this time, at Thanksgiving, Elizabeth and I sat at our aunt's house in Washington, D.C., tense and polite, while the grown-ups became slowly drunk.* Jill remembers how she and her sister and cousins played football outside in the November cold to escape the grown-ups' discussions, initially good-natured then turning hostile, or so it seemed to them, as the day wore on. They did not know the word *alcoholic* then, only saw that martinis and Old-Fashioneds and bottles of French wine at dinner made the adults cranky, which threatened their pleasure in being together with cousins for the holidays. Here, in Mexico, the palm trees, the heat, the ocean, the rich mysteries of Spanish and indigenous cultures fascinate and distract Jill from the past. She faces forward, dizzied by looking behind her at Elizabeth as they travel these bumpy roads.

When they arrive at the *casa*, the palm trees give her cousin's house above the Bay of Banderas a romantic, movie-set feeling, the only sounds waves breaking below on the beach and the voices of the chil-dren playing in the sand.

A Chinese woman, the children's nanny, hands Elizabeth her infant, whose name is also Jill. The other houseguests — the orthopedic surgeon and his red-haired wife, the dress designer and her guitar-playing husband — emerge from their rooms to hear about our trip to the plant nursery. The children come up from the beach to jump into the turquoise infinity pool on the terrace.

Elizabeth nurses the baby in the living room, open on three sides and covered with a giant roof of palms, called a *palapa*, where she sits in a woven leather chair admiring the pink bougainvillea and yellow *cupo de oro* espaliered up a black wrought-iron grill. Green philodendron vines hang from huge stone window boxes sculpted into the walls. *It is beautiful here,* Jill thinks. *The air is soft and the other houseguests are pleasant. No one is loud or drinking too much. Why do I feel lost? Because they are rich? Because everyone is straight, except for Sylvie? Or is it because no one really talks to each other, and I fear I'll disclose too much and embarrass myself or my cousin. Still, Sylvie is not straight and seems to enjoy the group. Perhaps that is because she drinks alcohol and hopes to design the garden of the doctor's vacation home in Napa and the guitar player's music studio in Mill Valley. Sylvie is more like them than me.*

Silently, Jill walks to the room she is sharing with Sylvie. *If I were drinking, I wouldn't feel so nervous. They can relax with their margaritas and Coronas, piña coladas and sangria. Alcohol smooths over the rough edges and self-consciousness, ensuring camaraderie. I can only sip lemonade and Pellegrino and ask them questions about themselves as I try to be part of the group.*

It is not just the wealth that makes Jill feel different. It is the hole in her heart from her mother's death and Vanessa's affairs and Margo moving back to New York and Pip's marriage to Marcia. It is being alone, in this dream house, without a real friend. Even her cousin is like quicksand. Jill never really knows where she stands with her. Is she important to Elizabeth or a charity case? She flips on the overhead fan, parting the white mosquito netting that drapes the bed and lies down.

"Jill?" Sylvie stands in the doorway, glistening with sweat, her red visor pushed back off her forehead, in her matching red outfit and red Crocs. "What are you doing?"

"Hiding."

Sylvie laughs. "From whom?"

"The doctor and his wife. And the children."

"I'll hide with you." Sylvie drops onto the bed, placing her visor and clipboard on the end table. "I've never been so hot." She kicks off her Crocs, even removes her starchy shorts, stretching her tan legs in front of her. Jill sees that her bra and underpants and even her watchband are red.

"How do you do that? Get everything to match?"

Sylvie laughs. "It's not hard. Is it too much?" She looks down at her red underwear.

"It's great," Jill says.

"I'm so glad we're not flying to Guadalajara tomorrow. Now we can have fun."

Jill nods. "Four hours of plant shopping was enough for me."

Sylvie wipes the sweat from her face, her spiked, streaked hair drenched. She holds her stomach. "Whoa. I feel like I'm rocking."

Jill reaches for the liter of bottled water on the bedstand. "Drink this. You're dehydrated."

"I think I am." Sylvie swallows some water and sighs.

They lie side by side, Sylvie, gazing at the ceiling, Jill returning to her book, a sad novel about a California childhood, written by a friend. But she cannot focus because she is not used to lying on the same bed with an attractive, half-naked woman who is not her lover. Elizabeth ran out of beds for this house party and apparently decided that Jill and Sylvie should share a bed because they are both lesbians and came without partners. Jill has barely slept since they arrived, afraid she might touch Sylvie although wanting to touch Sylvie.

"Aren't you hot?" Sylvie mops her forehead.

"I like the heat." Jill is afraid to look at Sylvie. "Beats being cold at Thanksgiving."

Sylvie leans back against the headboard. "Mexicans don't celebrate Thanksgiving, do they?"

"No Puritans and Wampanoags here," Jill laughs.

Sylvie glances at Jill oddly. "Is something wrong?"

Jill chews her lip. "Having fun is harder than I realized."

Sylvie rolls onto her side so that she is facing Jill. "Why?"

It is difficult for Jill not to stare at Sylvie's red lace bra and red bikini underpants. "I'm not drinking. That could be part of it."

"God, that's right," Sylvie says, as if she's never thought of this. "No margaritas or piña coladas. Poor baby."

Jill laughs and slugs some water. "I'm pale and uncool and stone cold sober."

Sylvie laughs. "You're cool, Jill. None of them have written books."

"The doctor and his wife look right through me."

"What?"

"As if I don't exist. Maybe because I'm a lesbian and don't live in Pacific Heights or have a weekend place in Napa."

"Don't knock it," Sylvie laughs. "I'm hoping to landscape their house in Napa. What a *coup* that would be."

Jill laughs.

Sylvie fans herself with a copy of *Vanity Fair*. "The thing is, Jill, anyone can see that Elizabeth loves you more than any of us. You're the one she laughs with. You have the past together, no matter how different your lives are now. She wants to share her luxuries with you. Can't you just enjoy them?"

Jill rubs her eyes. "I'm trying."

"Stop trying and let's do it." Sylvie squints outside, at the rustling palms above their balcony. "We'll go for a swim. You'll forget about feeling uncool and unloved." She opens the walnut wardrobe to find her bathing suit.

On the beach, Sylvie rubs Jill's back with sunblock before they swim to the wooden platform where the kayaks and Zodiac are hitched. The others stay up at the pool. *It is too bad*, Jill thinks, *that Sylvie is married to Joyce, who couldn't come because she is taking depositions for a big case.*

Banderas Bay is blue and salty and refreshing. Jill and Sylvie float on their backs, looking back at the white stucco house with its orange tile roof and palm trees and the huge palapa over the living room. They can hear the bass notes of the reggae music that Elizabeth and her husband blast from the stereo most of the day.

"We're lucky to be here," Jill says finally.

"Now you've got it." Sylvie splashes her.

"It's more fun with you," Jill says, feeling her breath catch. Something brushes against her toe. She hopes it is not a shark.

Sylvie makes neat kicks on her back, splashing further out into the bay. "I wish Darling were here. She would love this place."

"She would," Jill says, not wanting to think about Sylvie's partner, whom Sylvie always refers to as "Darling." Jill fights the sadness. She knows it is silly to feel disappointment of any kind in this paradise where everything is taken care of for her, and everything is beautiful. At the *casa*, she can see Jorge watering the plants along the deck in his white pants and colorful embroidered shirt. He stops, looks up, and waves to them.

"We can have plenty of fun without Darling," Sylvie says suddenly.

"Sure," Jill says, wondering what she means exactly.

"You and I have to do everything ecstatically so that when Darling and I come back in February to check on the landscaping, I can show her what's fun, and we can skip anything that's less than perfect. We'll do the research, you and I. Ok?"

"Absolutely," Jill smiles, afraid to mention the research she'd like to do.

In the morning, Elizabeth, in a white gown with a colorful embroidered smock and gold necklace, brings them coffee in bed, the baby, Jillie, slung on her hip.

"Get in with us," Sylvie says, patting the mattress. The three women and the baby lie together, the ceiling fan swirling lazily above them, the mosquito netting pulled back. They laugh about the doctor's wife, who regrets not buying the embroidered dress she fell in love with yesterday at the *mercado*. It made her look pale and fat, she said.

"I'm the same way," Jill laughs. "Like J. Alfred Prufrock. *Do I dare to eat a peach Do I dare to wear my trousers rolled?* That kind of thing."

"Well, stop it right now," her cousin laughs. "You're perfect as you are." She leaps up, baby in her arms. "You need to move. We all do."

Elizabeth decides they must all do her Jane Fonda workout, in what her husband calls "the penthouse," where she and her husband stay, away from their guests below and the dormitory for the children. The penthouse has sliding glass doors onto a porch overlooking the bay, and wide wooden beams across the ceiling. Pink bougainvillea laces the iron railing of the deck, which stretches the length of their suite.

"Ready?" Elizabeth, in a pink leotard and pink tights, adjusts some stereo dials behind a screen as the voice of Jane Fonda begins to roar over the speakers, drowning out the Reggae coming from another part of the house. Elizabeth winks at Jill, and, perfectly erect and proportioned in her costume, stares out at the ocean, leading them like a seasoned aerobics teacher, through the mambo and revolving doors and straddle-step routines that she appears to have practiced many times before. Sylvie yelps and giggles as she follows Elizabeth's and Jane Fonda's throaty encouragement. Sylvie was born for aerobics, with her narrow waist and strong, upright back, her bouncy knees and quick feet.

"Come on, Jill," yells Elizabeth. "Get those arms up. Keep your head back and shoulders tall." Elizabeth's graceful movements remind Jill of high school, of twenty-five years ago, when Elizabeth choreographed a chorus line for the senior class review at their all-girls school. Elizabeth cast Jill as a boy in the chorus line, along with six other girls who played boys, and in the final scene from *Hello, Dolly!*, the curviest girl in the class ended the dance perched on Jill's knee, which made Jill blush each time they rehearsed. Had Elizabeth known how frightened that scene she'd choreographed made Jill? Had she known then that Jill preferred women? *"Dance is like dreaming with your feet,"* Jill thinks, trying to remember who'd said that. *Was it Martha Graham? No. She called dance "the hidden language of the soul."*

The doctor's wife appears at the top of the stairs, watching longingly. Jill wishes she would disappear.

"Join us," Sylvie says, making room in the line for her.

"I'm such a klutz," says the doctor's wife. "I'll break an arm or something." But she steps in line between Jill and Sylvie, raising her arms and prancing with the rest of them as the sun rises behind them over the mountains, filling the room with hot, rosy light.

There is so much more to you than meets the eye, cries Jane Fonda, causing Sylvie to squeal and Margarita, Jorge's wife, younger than all of them, and much rounder, to pause as she removes coffee cups and wine glasses from the penthouse. A wistful smile on her face, she claps in time as the American *señoras* jiggle and pant and jump. Jill feels a wave of love for Margarita and suddenly pleasure in this motion together. They are four women fighting middle age in a beach house in Mexico, with Jane Fonda leading them in hand jives and heel-toe taps as the music pounds.

There is so much more to you than meets the eye, Jill repeats to herself as she lies on the white bed, cooled by the ceiling fan as she hides from the sun and people. She has almost finished the remarkable book by her friend from California. She would like to write the way her friend writes, layer on layer of past becoming present becoming past. She would like to have a brain like the writer's — funny and wise and clever. Or would she rather have a baby, like her cousin? Or a body like Sylvie's? Hating her restless discontent, she resolves to leave her mind in the swaying palms above the courtyard.

On their last night, Elizabeth's husband decides the adults will watch a movie in the penthouse while the children see *Ghostbusters II* downstairs in the bunkhouse. The Chinese nanny and the Mexican babysitter, a girl of fourteen, bring the children Pepsis and Mexican-flavored Dorito chips.

Upstairs, the grown-ups are watching *The Accidental Tourist*, about a travel writer who protects his readers from the inconveniences of foreign lands by providing tips on how to minimize direct contact with the countries they visit. Sylvie and Jill lie next to each other on the left side of Elizabeth's bed. The doctor and his wife are in the middle, and next to them Elizabeth nurses the baby on her breast while her husband paces restlessly, adjusting the satellite dish, the sound, and the picture quality.

Sylvie's body, pressed close to Jill's, makes Jill's stomach tingle. She glances at Sylvie, who appears not to notice, her head propped on a pillow, eyes following the movie intently. Her tan arm touches Jill's pale one again and again. Jill feels tingling and faint laughter in her stomach and wonders what it would be like to press her hands along those strong forearms that held the tow rope in the waves on the slalom ski today. To touch the hands that reached into the dark, wet soil to feel the texture of the garden dirt by the swimming pool. To hold the wrists that so easily performed the Jane Fonda doorknob twists during today's workout. Jill wonders if Sylvie feels this tingling as her chest rises and falls. She wonders if she will allow this desire that has been building between them to express itself. Layers of herself sharpen into focus.

The movie over, Jill and Sylvie go down to their room and now lie in their big bed under the bridal veil netting, the overhead fan murmuring as the sea breaks below.

"Are you awake?" Sylvie whispers.

Jill nods. "Yes."

Sylvie sits up. "I was thinking…" Jill waits. She can smell coconuts on Sylvie's skin and *tequila* on her breath. "Did you feel something, upstairs, watching the movie?"

Jill can see Sylvie's brown eyes, clear and intense, leaning toward her. "Feel something?" She doesn't want to make a mistake.

Sylvie moves so close her breath warms Jill's cheek. "When we were lying on your cousin's bed?"

"Yes," Jill says. "I felt it."

"I was turned on."

Jill shivers. "So was I."

"I've never felt that way before. I mean, you know, for you, about you."

Jill blushes. "I've been feeling it all week." There, she has said it. She hopes she does not sound too eager or needy although she feels she might burst from holding back so much desire.

They lie in silence. The moon is descending over Banderas Bay, its beams following them across the water and into the room. Jill's heart is pounding.

Sylvie takes her hand, making Jill's stomach dance. "It would be fun, wouldn't it?"

"Yes." Jill can hardly breathe. Sylvie's lips are nearly touching hers.

"I want to be naughty," Sylvie whispers, moving closer, crossing a leg over Jill's torso. "Darling doesn't have to know, does she?"

"She doesn't," Jill whispers, lifting onto her right elbow and staring down at Sylvie as the waves pound, reaching up to them, as the moon reaches down through the bridal veil in a glow of white.

"I've been wanting to do this," Sylvie says, her petite body pressing closer.

Jill laughs. "I wish you'd said."

"Now I have." She is moving on top of Jill. As their lips touch Jill places her hand on the tanned, flat stomach she has admired all week. Sylvie's lips taste of coconut and salt and plumeria and tequila. Jill does not feel worried or guilty, only excited. The betrayal of Darling is Sylvie's problem, not hers.

"Go down on me," Sylvie whispers.

If you *can make love to a woman under the full moon, life is not at so bad and sad,* Jill is thinking, her mouth on Sylvie's creamy erection. Sylvie's fingers tug gorgeously on Jill's hair. Jill is spreading Sylvie's legs wider, fingers teasing Sylvie's breasts. They are sloppy and hot and alive as a low, happy cry begins to vibrate in Sylvie's throat, moving out across the room and into the tropical night.

They breathe together, Jill kissing Sylvie's spiked, salty hair. Jill feels powerful holding Sylvie, whose knee is wedged between her legs, her fingers now finding the wet hard-on between Jill's legs. Seedlings are bursting through Jill's legs like red stalks of ginger; there are yellow hibiscus where Sylvie touches her; *cupo de oro* slicing Jill's stomach, where Sylvie presses her hip bone against Jill's. So many flowers open and blossom that Jill can't count them all. She knows suddenly that Elizabeth, too, wants to be touched this way, to feel this trembling and to express the longing that has existed between them since childhood, when they boxed half-naked in Jill's bedroom. She and Sylvie have unfurled their reserve. Perhaps Elizabeth will join them in the morning, give her baby to the nurse and cross the line of respectability, riding the wave as they are now, surfers gliding through the barrel. Sylvie's fingers are moving deeper inside, reminding Jill of Jorge, his package rising in his pants, making Jill shiver. Sylvie is Jorge entering Jill with his rough hands, inside her now, his hard-on blooming among Jill's jasmine and orchids and mangoes. Jill is losing track, cannot tell Sylvie from

Jorge, from the doctor's wife, from Elizabeth, from the touch of a woman, of a man.

Now Sylvie is begging Jill for more. "Dear God," she shouts, touching herself as Jill rides the spasms of swaying surf inside her.

"What fun," Sylvie says dreamily, half dozing, kissing Jill's hand when they have done. "So many visitors. Did you feel them all?"

"I did." Jill pulls Sylvie on top of her.

"Again?" They start over, crazier and freer, falling asleep in each other's arms.

"*Buenos dias, senoritas*," Elizabeth laughs, carrying a tray of coffee and rolls. "Ooolala," she says, seeing them naked and entwined. "Look at the lovely goddesses."

Sylvie smiles. "Can you join us?"

Elizabeth hesitates, takes a step forward, then stops, hearing the baby cry. "Rain check," she giggles, hurrying away.

When we are back at home, I will break this fear, Jill thinks. *Find a way to stop the anxiety.* She listens to the waves crashing below and the cries of children playing in the pool. She cherishes the calm, even breath of the woman in her arms. When she returns to California, she will learn Spanish, start a garden, and swim every day. When her photographs of Puerto Vallarta are processed, she will invite Sylvie to her cottage above the bay in Sausalito to commemorate their excursion into another country.

PAST LIVES

She lives in a suburb, and she is there now in her ranch house overlooking the coast oaks and the hayfields beyond. She walks among her appliances — her microwave, her washer and dryer, her Cuisinart, her stereo, and her remote-control TV — barefoot and naked, except for her red Jockey underpants.

"How many red Jockey underpants do you own?" I ask.

"I don't know. Maybe seven." Morgan sees my smile. "They don't show the bleeding so much." Her periods are war zones in which blood gushes, bursts, and spills.

She is in her house now, playing back the twenty-two phone messages that came while we soaked in the warm, steamy baths of Calistoga. There are messages from her seventeen-year-old daughter, who is staying in San Francisco with her grandmother; from her nineteen-year-old in New Mexico, who will marry a soldier in December; from her ex-husband in Berkeley, looking for the seventeen-year-old; from her friend Justine with news of a garage-sale nearby; from her business partner, who wonders if Morgan can be on first call; from her high school friend, Marianne, who suggested they have sex several years ago before she moved to Cleveland.

———

Calistoga means escape from phone calls. We wander from our room to the hot pools to the sauna and back to the room, where she presses me to the mattress with the same strong arms that catch babies from moaning mothers.

Her eyes are blue like a cat's, unblinking, and lined with dark lashes, top and bottom. I stare at her eyes till the clock melts, locked in her safe, unwavering gaze. She sees the black carp floating motionless in my heart but is not afraid of their unspoken admissions — my father's medical examinations; my mother's painted fingernails thrust down my throat.

I crawl up the calm of her legs to her breasts, and then to her mane, wild and gold. Her fingers caress my hair as she pulls my lips to hers. I am one of her garden plants, her blue lobelia, begging for water and sun.

"Make me pregnant," I whisper. She laughs, tugs tighter on my hair. "I want your baby," I say, wrapping my legs around her waist.

She laughs. "I've had two already. That's enough for me."

"I'll raise her," I say. "She will be wild and freckled and blue-eyed like you."

"You don't get to choose with children," she says. "You get what you get." Her lips, which are lavender-pink, touch mine. She rocks me, moves me, enters and reenters me. I want to marry her muscular shoulders and deep calm.

"Bite my nipples," she whispers.

I obey.

"Harder," she says.

"I'm afraid I'll hurt you."

"Hurt me a little."

I bite harder and she groans. Then I kiss the smooth skin along the side of her neck and chest. I dream I am her child now, the sibling of her seventeen-year-old who stretches so languidly on the sofa in the TV room of their ranch house watching show after show, waiting for her life to begin. I have never met my other sibling, who is learning how to heal with Chinese needles.

They are exotic, this woman and her daughters. Sometimes, when their mother holds me, she hums a song that has no tune; I drift back centuries, to the desert and ancient fires, to medicine women stirring potions in cauldrons beneath the moon.

"My bowels have frozen up," I tell her.

She looks at me, her fingers still inside me. "You can't poo?" *Poo* seems an oddly childlike word for a sorceress.

I nod. "I'm afraid I'll make gassy sounds around you. My bowels are locked."

She stares at the ceiling. "My bowels haven't moved either." I am surprised. She is such a natural woman. I thought her bowels would always move. Knowing this, I don't feel as embarrassed.

Sometimes, when she drives her car fast on the freeway, weaving through traffic, cruising for cops in the rearview mirror, she is my boyfriend. When she hauls my massage table to the car as if it were light as popcorn, she is my husband. She is my wife when she chops garlic and zucchini, broccoli and eggplant, tofu and scallions, then adds herbs, quietly creating a taste beyond heaven. She is my lover when I lie on top of her.

"I want to fuck you," I say to her.

She studies me a moment, widening her legs. "Go ahead."

"I want to lick you first, then fuck you," I say.

"Even better," she says, opening so that I can caress her with my tongue. I smell her pussy, fresh, like the sweetgrass baskets the gypsies in New Hampshire brought my mother in the summers. She rises and lifts to accept the slow, hard circles my tongue makes. She is hungry. I place her fingers on her clit to help me find the exact threads of pleasure she craves. Her cries build to a wail.

In the motel, after sex, our periods arrive at the exact same moment — red blood on the same white toilet paper. We both have cramps. We laugh and swallow Advil.

"I'll hypnotize you back to sleep," I say, counting slowly down from fifty, down deeper, down the staircase into the safe, dark earth. Her eyes close, her limbs twitch, her breath deepens, and she is gone. Next to her, I am hot, bloody, horny, and awake. Her snores startle, then arouse me.

"Sometimes I imagine you're a man," I say, when she wakes.

"I'm not," she says. "But you can imagine whatever you want." There are so many varieties of woman. Those who drive fast, who snore, who lift heavy things, who dance and teach and write and nurse and balance budget sheets. I fall asleep again, wet and aching, my head against her shoulder.

I sleep. I dream. I dream I am with Ellie, my ex, in her bathtub in Portola Valley. Ellie is on top of me, fucking me. It feels like swimming, like the gods sliding in and out of me, her breasts slurping against mine as she thrusts and presses. Her sweat drips on my face. She is coming, I am coming. I am afraid that her teenage son will discover us.

"He's in college, remember," she whispers, climbing deeper inside me.

"What about Cassandra?" Cassandra is the new lover she has left me for.

"She's at work." Ellie's dick is about to explode. What will I say to Morgan? I have promised I will tell her if there is someone else, and here I am, fucking Ellie, who is wild with desire in a way she's never been.

"Hello?" The door opens in the dream; a bright light shatters our eyes. Cassandra is standing over us, beautiful and serious, speaking with a crisp British accent. "What's happening here? I smell fire."

Ellie withdraws her penis and sits up. "We're looking for Tampax," she says with a charming smile. I stare down at our naked bodies; menstrual blood is smeared across our bellies.

Cassandra looks away. "I'll forget what I've seen." She closes the door quietly behind her.

I am breathless. "Is she angry?"

Ellie cocks her head. "She'll forget. She is blind."

But Morgan will mind. How will I explain this to her?

I wake up, heart thudding, lying in Morgan's arms. My cheek still rests on her shoulder. I have not betrayed her. I fall back to sleep.

In my next dream, I'm in the living room of the row house in Baltimore where I grew up. My mother, nearly bald, has come to visit wearing only her nightgown. Her hair is falling out from chemotherapy.

"Mom, is it really you? I thought you were dead." I am weeping with happiness to see her. I hold her thin body. "I've missed you so much."

"I'm here, Jill."

Her bony hand is warm. I hope she will not notice that Dad has changed the living room and has placed on the coffee table a photo of his new girlfriend, who has large breasts and is wearing a bikini; his arm is around her waist.

"What is it like to be dead?" I ask.

She smiles. "I don't know. Do you?"

I am crying harder. "Please, don't leave, Mom. Not yet."

I wake up. I am clutching Morgan's hand.

After the spa and the pools, we drive south, back to Morgan's house in Marin, which is painted red. "I want to see a picture of you in your hippie days," I say, as she unpacks. Morgan lived in Haight-Ashbury when she was eighteen, took acid and hung out at clubs like the Avalon and the Fillmore, helicoptered into Woodstock with the Grateful Dead, took LSD, lived in an ashram, wore flowers in her hair and hitchhiked to New York in a pot smuggler's airplane.

"Let me look for a picture," she says. Her younger daughter is still in San Francisco with her grandmother. Morgan finds several photo albums. We sit in the TV room, where she shows me a photo of herself laughing, in a ponytail, wearing a peasant dress with an embroidered top, walking barefoot in a mountain stream. I want to see more, so I take all the albums to the bedroom, lie down, and study her past. There are hundreds of photographs of people I don't know, of hippies in turbans and beards, of children and of Morgan. I realize how little I know her.

"Ah," she says, standing in the doorway as my eyes lock on one particular black-and-white photograph. "That's my wedding." She wears a white dress and white pants and a garland of flowers on her head; her eyes are closed as she sits in a circle, a bearded man, cross-legged, next to her. My heart lunges. I do not want to see this. I do not want to see her getting married to that man. I know it was taken twenty years ago, is only a distant memory now, but it was real then, and I am jealous. Still, I keep looking at these photographs of her past lives. I am reaching back into time, wishing I had been the one marrying Morgan.

I mustn't look anymore. I am becoming more withdrawn with each new image. My eyes stick again, this time to a close-up of Morgan, forehead taut, teeth clenched, neck muscles bulging, eyes closed.

"Allie's birth," she laughs. I inhale. Allie is her older daughter. Morgan's breasts are engorged; her knees are bent and spread wide; a woman leans over her. A dark, wet head is poking out of her vagina. The camera is so close you can see the hairs on Morgan's legs — only her name is not Morgan, it is Sajna — and she is naked except for socks, as seven people look down at her. I turn away, turn back, to another photo in the sequence. Morgan is exhausted and pale, touching the cheek of the bearded man, who is holding the new baby with unspeakable tenderness. All the people watching are wearing white turbans.

I want to be that man who is holding the baby. I want to be the father and the husband. *Close the book,* I tell myself. *Don't look anymore.* But I open again. Now Morgan/Sajna is pregnant again, walking in her turban with the erect posture of a goddess. Her husband is also in white, in a turban. He is a yogi and head of the ashram, she explains, and she is a yogini. I have left my body, am wandering alone and estranged as Morgan explains another photo — "That is Simran Singh, who ran the ashram in New Mexico. That is Tatshavi, who lived in L.A. Those are my daughters with our spiritual teacher."

Is this a cult, I wonder. Do I dare ask?

There are so many husbands and wives and boyfriends and yogis and yoginis that I am leaving my body. *You're OK*, I hear the shrink in Philadelphia tell me. *It was wrong for your father to examine you, even if he was a doctor.* I am marching down Fifth Avenue in New York with thousands of lesbians and gay men, shouting "We're here, we're queer, get used to it," in my first Lesbian/Gay Pride parade. *You have a right to be free*, Margo is telling me as we eat steak salad at the Buffalo Roadhouse on Seventh Avenue soon after we told my parents I'm a lesbian. *You've done nothing wrong.* My father's eyes are sad; my mother is crying. I am afraid to touch or be touched. I am an outlaw, outside the mainstream, outside the outside.

"Jill?" Morgan moves closer. "What's wrong?"

I can't talk. I am ashamed and angry and guilty. "Nothing," I say.

Morgan pushes the photos books away. "Come on," she whispers. Her touch is reassuring. "You've seen enough."

"I feel like an alien."

She puts the albums back on the shelf. "This is the past. I'm different now. So are you, I'm guessing."

"I want to see, but when I see, I feel left out and alone."

She pulls me closer on the sofa. "I love you, you know. You're not an alien."

She loves me. I am frozen. What is wrong with me? I feel desire in my legs but ice everywhere else. The photos have taken me away from Morgan; I thought they'd bring us closer. She is a stranger in her white turban married to a yoga man, a Jew born in Brooklyn, with a seven-syllable Indian name. She is my father with a blood pressure cuff and an otoscope checking my groin for swollen glands; she is my mother begging me not to be a lesbian. She is a cross-legged witch on a high plain in New Mexico eating tofu and brown rice, chanting hypnotic verses.

"Jill? Talk to me?" "

"I can't."

"Why?"

"Hold me," I whisper.

She covers me with a blanket and rocks me in her arms. We lie in silence. My eyes are closed.

"What's happening?" The wall clock emits a strange hum.

"I don't know."

"Is it so bad?"

"Sometimes," I say.

"What are you feeling?" Her eyes puzzle over me.

I inhale. I want to hide. I'm ashamed. I make myself speak. I have promised Morgan the truth. "I am jealous of your past and remembering my own. The scary things with my parents. Lines crossed."

"The photographs triggered memories?" she asks softly.

I nod. "Made me jealous. Of your husband and your children and your past. And there were things that happened with my father."

"Our love-making triggered them?"

I nod *yes*. I'm embarrassed. I feel like dying.

"Jill," she says. "Talk to me."

"They come back. During sex sometimes."

She gets up, brings me a glass of water.

"Not always," I say. "I never know."

She nods quietly. At least she is not angry. I can feel her grounding herself, sending her taproot down into the earth. "You know, I left my ex-husband years ago, and the ashram well before that. I left because I didn't respect our teacher anymore, and there were too many rules. His rules. I'm here with you now. No one else is here. No men, no parents, no ex-husbands, no children. Just me. Don't do anything that makes you uncomfortable."

I hear the words, but I cannot feel them. I am lost in my past, lost in my fantasy of *her* past.

She strokes my hair. "The people and events from our past have led us to each other. That's a good thing."

I try to blink away the bearded man and my parents and the memories that choke me when I feel close and sexy. "I wish I were as generous as you."

She smiles, her blue-green eyes gentle, her freckles lovely and kind. "We can work this out, Jill. We can talk to each other. We can hold each other. Does it have to be so tragic?"

"It might be," I say with a tiny smile.

She smiles back, reaching for my armpits. "You need a good tickle."

"No, please." But she is tickling me with the strong hands that catch babies, and I am laughing.

"Freckle, flower, friend," I say, and with the words, the love returns and the memories fade. They will come back again, I know. But right now, I'm better, freer. Morgan has coaxed me down off the ledge. She has blue eyes and freckled cheeks, is funny and wise and beautiful. The others are gone. If they come back, when they come back, I will tell her.

BENEATH MY DIGNITY TO CLIMB
A TREE

"Were you a tomboy?" I ask Morgan. We are watching *Seinfeld*, the "Outing" episode where George and Jerry's parents read that their sons are gay, which they aren't, of course. It's a funny and diverting episode, when it's hideously hot, as it is today, maybe ninety-five degrees outside.

"What?" Morgan asks, pressing the TV *pause* button. She's had a long day at her office, and one of her expectant mothers has just called to say that her contractions have started, which usually means Morgan will be up all night at a birth. For now, she's in what she calls "slug" mode, saving her energy for the night ahead.

"A friend of mine is editing a book on tomboys and asked for submissions. Which started me thinking. Were you a tomboy?"

Morgan sips a non-alcoholic beer. "Are you a tomboy if you had a pet snake and a go-cart and loved playing doctor with your friend Suzanne?"

I perk up. "Like kissing her?"

"Kissing and..." she hesitates. "Lots of other stuff. We more or less had sex every day after school."

"Wow. Lucky you."

"It was great until our mothers busted us."

"Did you get punished?"

"Sort of. We weren't ever allowed to hang out again at each other's houses." Morgan clicks *Seinfeld* back on.

"My tomboy wasn't man enough to kiss a girl." I stare down at my pale arms. "Do you see the tomboy in me now?"

"The tomboy in you?" She blinks at me. "Your clothes are kind of..." she trails off.

"What about my clothes?"

She pauses the show with a sigh. "You buy men's clothes. Men's khaki pants and shirts. You hardly ever buy women's stuff. You dress like your father."

I flinch. "I bought that tie-dye dress at the music festival."

"But will you ever wear it?" She unpauses the TV. Seinfeld's father is blaming his wife for turning Jerry gay ("Not that anything is wrong with that," he says) because she dressed him in shorts that looked like culottes.

I take the clicker from her hand and press *pause* again. "Can we have a little more discussion about this?"

Morgan rubs her eyes. "You discuss. I'll listen."

I settle into the couch and stare down at her muscular, suntanned legs. "I wanted to *be* Peter Pan as a kid."

"Didn't we all?"

"Some people wanted to be Wendy. Vanessa did."

"Oh, well. Vanessa," Morgan laughs.

"Did you want to grow up into a woman?"

"I knew I didn't want to be a man." Morgan eyes the clicker restlessly.

I think back, trying to understand. "I wanted to *be* Peter and come home to Wendy every night. If Mary Martin could do it, I thought I could, too. I tried to will my body into arrested development."

"How?" Morgan looks interested.

"I'd stand in front of my bedroom mirror in my white Carter's Spanky pants and my white Carter's undershirt and pray I'd stay flat-chested and curve-free. I swore it would never be beneath my dignity to climb a tree."

Morgan rubs a hand through her short wavy hair, which she has dyed red. I would never dye my hair red. "When my hormones kicked in, and I discovered boys, my lesbian phase ended."

"My lesbian phase never ended." I am looking at a Mexican terra cotta sculpture on the bookshelf of a baby emerging from a woman's womb. Morgan has a lot of these statue things around the house that clients and friends and family give her. Now they give us dachshund ceramics because we have two long-haired doxies. "It wasn't that I thought being a girl was bad, it just wasn't right for me. I wanted to stay a boy and marry Kim Novak."

"I'd forgotten about Kim Novak. She was a babe."

"I would have settled for Sophia Loren or Shirley MacLaine or Debi Reynolds."

"You thought Debi Reynolds was sexy?"

I nod. "One night when I was about ten, my friend Lois spent the night, and I tried to teach her how to fantasize about rescuing movie stars in distress, like Debi Reynolds."

"What?" Morgan rolls her eyes.

"Lois was the smartest girl in our class, and I thought it would be easy for her to learn to fantasize with me about rescuing Debi Reynolds from a villain. We'd gallop up on our palominos, grab Debi by the waist, and lift her away from the bad cowboy at high speed, then put our arms around her and canter off into the sunset."

Morgan laughs. "Lois couldn't get into it?"

I shake my head. "She really tried, but she didn't feel the joy. I forgot all about that until we were eighteen at a debutante party and she took me aside to tell me how much she'd appreciated my trying to teach her how to rescue Debi Reynolds on a horse. We got a good laugh."

"You're nuts." Morgan sips her near-beer. "Can we go back to *Seinfeld*?"

"Just a little longer," I plead. "Because I began to think something was wrong with me, that being a girl who wanted to be a boy and marry a girl and rescue a movie star was really, really bad."

Seinfeld is on again. Now George's parents are freaking out, and I'm remembering, how, when, when I was a kid and professional boxing was always being broadcast on TV, my mother's friend Genevieve gave my sister and me two sets of boxing gloves that her sons didn't want. One weekend when our cousins Mary Lou and Elizabeth stayed over, my sister and Mary Lou and I decided that Elizabeth and I should have a boxing prizefight in our underwear. My sister was Lizzie's coach, and Mary Lou was mine. They dabbed Mom's Blue Grass after-bath cologne on our shoulders and urged us out from our "corners" into combat. Lizzie, definitely not a tomboy, did not find the experience as fabulous as the three of us did. She and I never actually hit each other, just sort of bumped and pushed each other around, raising our gloves triumphantly into the air and claiming victory when my sister rang the bell at the end of each round. When we suggested a rematch on other visits, Elizabeth refused, and I never found another willing opponent.

There were other tomboy activities I could enjoy by myself, like playing in the treehouse in the backyard or throwing stones at the Rouse boys or making dams in the polluted creek behind our house. On special occasions, my sister would join me on the roof of the corporation-yard garages, where only the neighborhood boys dared go because the place was creepy and smelled of urine, and the rusty drainpipes we had to climb were dangerously loose. But once up there, we could gaze down at the earth with a momentary sense of freedom from family, school, and church.

Unlike Morgan, my same-sex crushes on girls and women did not disappear when I hit puberty. They got worse. I longed to embrace the junior high school secretary, the bouncy cheerleaders with the big smiles, the beautifully busty field hockey coach. Chasing and retrieving balls in sports was the only activity that allowed my inner tomboy space to breathe.

Meanwhile, my tyrannical superego viewed my inner tomboy as a menace to be extinguished. I slammed the door on her/him, not allowing them out until I was twenty-six, half-crazy with longing.

The *Seinfeld* episode is over. Happy heterosexuality is restored. "Do you think tomboys are precursors to butch lesbians? Or transsexuals?" I say.

Morgan turns off the TV. "We're still on that?"

"Do you think most tomboys become lesbians?"

Morgan sighs. "I didn't become a lesbian until after I'd been straight for twenty years and had two children."

"But you had your little friend Suzanne."

"We had fun. But I still don't understand why it matters so much to you if a tomboy becomes a butch lesbian or a femme lesbian or straight or something else altogether."

I want Morgan to like probing these sexuality issues as much as I do, but too much analysis makes her crazy, especially when she is facing an all-nighter. "I care because my identity is wrapped up in my sexuality. Yours, too, I'm guessing."

Morgan touches my arm. "OK, here's my final answer: Some of us want to be a man sometimes and a woman at other times, and it's all OK. Why wouldn't a woman want to be a man some of the time? Men have more freedom, they can roam around at night and not be afraid of getting assaulted, and they have more power. They make the laws and run the world."

"But I want to be a man a lot of the time. And it's not just their power I want. Sometimes I want a penis. I want to know what it feels like to be inside a woman. What it feels like to fuck."

"Wouldn't that be fun?" Morgan laughs.

"Does it bother you that you'll never know?"

Morgan shrugs. "Not enough to change sexes." Morgan closes her eyes, then opens them. "Do you think you would have chosen to be a boy if things had been different when you were a kid, like they are today, when gender is more fluid?"

I inhale.

"Several of my pregnant mothers have given birth to babies with ambiguous genitalia. Doctors used to decide what sex the child would be and they—"

"Chopped off their penises?"

"To put it crudely, yes. Usually with the parents' consent. It's a lot easier to make a boy into a girl than make a girl into a boy. They thought if they did it early, the kids would embrace the gender their parents chose for them."

"But..."

"But now parents of intersex kids try to leave them alone and let the kids decide when they're older."

"It's complicated."

She puts an arm around me. "I love you, you know. Just the way you are. However you are. Personally, I'm glad you don't have a penis. I had a husband with one, and it was a real pain sometimes."

"You don't miss it?"

"No!" she cries, taking my hand.

I go to the kitchen and pour us each a glass of sparkling water. "I'd like to make a toast."

"Great."

"To our tomboys," I say.

"To our tomboys," Morgan smiles. "Who have made us the women we are today."

EX-LOVERS' WEEKEND

Margo, who is married to Ellen, is having a heart-to-heart with Sarah in this rented beach house in the Hamptons that Sarah has procured so that all of us have a chance to say goodbye to Margo.

Although Ellen agreed to the weekend gathering, she now seems to regret spending so much time with four of Margo's exes — Sarah, Lana, Betty and me. She is furiously yanking Pellegrino, Diet Pepsi, beer cans and wine bottles from a red plastic trash barrel under the kitchen sink and tossing them into separate bins with a clatter that competes with Lana and Betty's delighted squeals from the bedroom. Although they've known each other for decades, Lana and Betty have recently fallen in love and have spent much of the weekend in bed.

"Aluminum has to be separated from glass," Ellen is shouting, "and glass from plastic, and paper from all of it." A wine bottle shatters in one of the bins. "We won't be ready for the trash pick-up tomorrow if I'm the only one doing this. Has anyone read the landlord's rules besides me?"

I am pretending to read a book because when Ellen gets in this mood, it is best to leave her alone; diplomacy is crucial. The wrong inflection can trigger a full-blown meltdown. The source of Ellen's problem, I know, is that Sarah and Margo are alone in the bedroom having the "talk" that Ellen herself insisted they have when she conducted a seance last night. Now Ellen is angry that they've been in the bedroom so long. I try to practice *metta*, sending loving kindness to Ellen because I know she is exhausted from keeping Margo alive as the cancer spreads, causing Margo to waste and shrivel like an old woman although she is only fifty-four. My *metta* is not working well. I am as furious at Ellen as she is with us. Despite her efforts to be nice to us, she is driving all of us crazy.

"Maybe after dinner we can do the recycling together," I suggest mildly, closing the copy of *How to Choose Your New Dog* that I have found on the cottage bookshelf.

"Right," Ellen says, slamming a cabinet.

"Did you know that every dog has a unique nose print?" I say, hoping to distract Ellen. "It's like a fingerprint you can use it to identify a dog." Morgan and I have discussed adopting another dachshund, but Morgan now says she will die before bringing another stubborn, yappy, hard to-train wiener dog into our home.

Ellen curses under her breath, kicking the bins toward to the door with such rage that I am grateful she and Margo turned their handguns in to the police several years ago. Margo confided this to me one day, after one of their "humdingers," as Ellen, who is from the Midwest, calls their fights. They both feared they might shoot each other if they kept weapons in the house.

With the garbage-wrestling now relocated to the front porch, I rinse and dry the lettuce for the salad, turning on the CD of Keith Jarrett's *Koln Concert*, whose melodic piano improvs I haven't heard since that terrible year in San Francisco when I left Margo for Vanessa. Vanessa's boyfriend Dean played Keith Jarrett the night Vanessa and I overdosed on LSD, and the music soothed us. The emotional turmoil today makes me miss Morgan, who's back in California. I try to think if she's at home today or has office hours or is taking a hike with a friend. I'll call anyway because I need her pasta puttanesca recipe, which I had hoped to make for dinner tonight. On the other hand, we probably don't have the right ingredients at this rental house — certainly not the anchovies — so I'll do a stir-fry again.

I'm glad Morgan didn't come on this trip now that Ellen has gone off the deep end. Last night Ellen insisted on holding a séance, claiming to be clairvoyant and promising to contact Margo's beloved friend Deena, who died suddenly of a stroke three months ago. Last night, Ellen "contacted" Deena, who "had a message for Margo" -- she must be more transparent with her feelings, particularly with Ellen, and also with Sarah. But the "transmission" ended when Deena/Ellen became so critical of Margo that Sarah, our hostess, insisted we stop the seance, triggering an asthma episode that required Ellen be transported to the ER in Southampton.

We have all been walking on eggshells today. What would really help me now is some of that wine the others have been guzzling, but I haven't had a drink in years, and I don't want to start. A walk or a swim would help, but I've had three swims and two walks already today, and someone needs to make dinner.

"Can I help?" Lana, who's become a famous magazine editor, is standing in the doorway, all soft and pink, brushing her light brown hair contentedly after her afternoon in bed with Betty, who once cut the hair of every lesbian in Greenwich Village before becoming psychotherapist. Betty was Margo's lover between Lana and Sarah and sometime before Deena and me and Ellen.

"What is Ellen *doing*?" Lana asks, nibbling a piece of raw zucchini.

"Taking out the garbage."

"God, she's loud."

"Who's loud?" Ellen has reentered the room, her breathing labored.

"You are, my darling," Lana laughs, ruffling Ellen's neatly combed hair.

Ellen looks gorgeous, so tanned and healthy, with her brown eyes, short wavy brown hair, blue and white striped cotton sailor's jersey and white shorts that it's hard to think of her as a sickly asthmatic. Margo *used* to look that way, too — preppy and crisp and very J. Crew — but cancer has made her clothes baggy, her head bald and her pale cheeks hollow. Her stunning blue eyes seem to pop from her head as she gets closer to death. I can't look too hard at her because it makes me too sad to see her in this state. She shouldn't be dying. She is too young, too wonderful, too talented, too kind and funny and generous to die. But two years ago she discovered a lump in her abdomen, and told no one, especially not her doctor, and now the cancer has gone to her brain. It is just a matter of time.

Ellen is watching me chop veggies. "You shouldn't have to cook, Jill. You cooked last night." She glares at Lana, who is now thumbing through a *New Yorker* on the couch. "Everyone should take turns cooking."

"Betty," Lana calls. "Come help Jill make dinner." Lana tosses down the magazine. "Betty, come help cook!" she calls again, turning to Jill. "Betty worked at vegetarian restaurant in the East Village before she went to beauty school."

"She doesn't seem to like cooking as much as you think," Ellen says, setting the table. Lana disappears into the bedroom.

Ellen winks at me. "Betty's way too hot and bothered to make dinner."

"Well, they're new," I say. I actually don't mind cooking. It gives me something to do beside worry about Margo. Besides, it's dangerous to look idle around Ellen.

"Do you think Sarah and Margo are still talking?" Ellen glances down the hallway toward the room where Sarah and Margo are caucusing.

"What did you want them to talk about?" I find some eggplant in the fridge and decide to add that to the stir fry.

"Did Margo tell you what happened with Sarah and Zoe?"

"Who's Zoe?" I say, putting down the knife.

Ellen steps closer. "Sarah's ex." A slightly demonic smile lights her face. "You've never met her?"

"Don't think so," I say, looking through the spice drawer for something to liven up the veggies.

Ellen massages her hands. "Zoe was Sarah's student at B.U., twenty years younger and an alcoholic. Sarah played Big Mama to her, paid Zoe's tuition and medical bills and bought her a car." Ellen begins wiping the counter, which is already spotless. "She has a thing for younger women."

"Does she?" I say, wondering if I'm too old for Sarah. I felt a kind of electric charge with Sarah at lunch today, but maybe I made it up. I definitely need to call Morgan tonight, get myself grounded.

Ellen has spotted some dirt in a dark slot between the refrigerator and the stove and is probing it with a broom. "We stopped seeing Sarah because of Zoe. You're sure Margo didn't tell you?'

"There's a lot she doesn't tell me."

Ellen comes closer. "Sarah and Zoe came down from Boston to see us one weekend, and Zoe drank about a fifth of Scotch after Sarah and I went to bed."

"Never heard about this," I say, spotting some tarragon in the cabinet.

"Margo got drunk, too, and Zoe started sobbing, telling Margo that she was in love with her and started kissing Margo right there on the couch, in *our* house." Ellen's eyes widen into full-blown shock.

"Margo stopped drinking years ago."

"She had stopped. And she has again, of course, because of the cancer," Ellen says. "But we went through a rough patch a couple of years ago. Financially, with... It doesn't matter, the point is, Margo was drunk but not shitfaced. Not like Zoe, who announced she was in love with Margo."

"Everyone falls in love with Margo," I say. "Everyone in this house did. She's pretty wonderful."

"Not in *my* house, they don't fall in love with Margo." Ellen thrusts the broom into the closet.

"Did you and Sarah and Zoe and Margo resolve things?"

Ellen picks up a sponge, wiping the counters again. "Took years. I sent Sarah and Zoe packing as soon as Margo told me what happened." Ellen sprays Windex on the refrigerator door. "I let Sarah know that she and Zoe were no longer welcome in our house and never would be as long as they were still together."

"What did Margo say?" Sarah and Margo had been friends for decades.

"Oh, Margo was all set to forgive Zoe." Ellen reddens. "You know how she is. 'She didn't mean it, Ellen,' she tried to tell me. And Sarah blew it off, too. Tried to say it was nothing. And Zoe didn't even remember she'd made a pass at Margo because she had a blackout." Ellen pushes up the sleeves of her striped jersey as she pumps Windex into the garbage can. "I was hoping we'd never see Sarah again, but a year later, she calls Margo out of the blue and says she and Zoe have split up, and she'd like to come see us. See Margo, really. Margo had just gotten the cancer diagnosis, and we needed help, and the truth is, Sarah's been an angel, took care of the dogs when Margo had that second surgery and paid for our train tickets and hotel room at the Waldorf so we could go to Deena's memorial."

"Wow," I say. "How generous."

"When she wants something."

I glance at the door to the bedroom to be sure Sarah and Margo are still inside. "What did Sarah want?"

"Margo, of course."

"Not sexually?" I say, incredulous.

"No, no. She wanted the friendship back." Ellen is quiet for a minute, absently picking lint off her T-shirt. "I tell you, Jill, Margo has some screwed-up friends, and Sarah tops the list." Ellen pulls her asthma inhaler from her pocket, inserting the plastic proboscis into her mouth.

I scratch my head. "Zoe must have been really drunk to flirt like that."

Ellen throws a sponge into the sink. "She mauled Margo."

I can't help laughing. Mistake.

"It wasn't funny, Jill. How would you like it if a friend of yours came on to Morgan that way?"

"Morgan's pretty good at saying no," I say. "I'm the one who's had had problems in that department."

"Don't remind me." Ellen cracks open a new sponge from the cellophane. "You and Morgan both got all nutty about that Japanese butch with the strap-on."

"The three of us had a lot of fun."

"Jesus." Ellen shakes her head. "If Margo tried to get me in a three-way, I'd kill her."

"You'd miss her if you killed her," I say, amazed that Ellen has forgotten that she and Margo and I had a three-way in my bed years ago, when she and Margo were new, and we were struggling for a way for all of us to be friends. It had been a disaster. Ellen seemed to have fun but had a temper tantrum after, and I was way too nervous to let go. Margo was the only one who got off. *Goddess bless Margo!*

Ellen bangs a fist on the counter. "All of you Margo-exes think she walks on water. But, I tell you, Jill, she's no saint. She lures people in, makes them feel special, sends them birthday cards and thank-you notes and does favors for them, designs their business cards and their book jackets and anything else they need and doesn't charge them a penny."

"She designed my new business card," Jill says guiltily.

"She designed a whole magazine for Lana, and you know how Lana paid her? Sent her some pears from Harry & David. I hate pears."

I laugh. *You should be grateful, Ellen,* I think to myself. *Margo has supported you for twenty years.*

"'That's what any friend would do, hun,' Margo tells me. 'I'm happy to do it.' She denies that these people are taking advantage of her. Or that they're in love with her."

I remember well Margo's effect on people, remember my own jealousy, in my weaker moments, of her ability to turn a group of strangers into her best friends. "She genuinely likes people," I say. "You and I are more —"

"She *doesn't* like people." Ellen pulls some plastic dinner plates from the cupboard and slaps them on the counter. "She hates them."

"Who does she hate? Nobody I can think of."

"Bullshit," she sighs, shaking her head.

"Dinner," I yell, hoping the meal will nip this potential meltdown in the bud. Betty and Lana emerge quickly from the bedroom, hair mussed again, cheeks glowing. Margo limps down the hall smiling, holding Sarah's arm.

"Did you conquer the recycling, Ellen?" Sarah asks in her Southern drawl. "Sounded a missile attack." She picks up a plate and serves herself some stir-fry. "Thank you for suggesting that Margo and I talk. We shared some lovely memories of a road trip we took one summer in Margo's MG. Drove down to my parents' house in Mississippi. She'd never seen that part of the South."

"Eye-opener," Margo says, shaking her head, sitting down at the table and picking up one of the dachshunds.

"She couldn't get over the 'Colored' fountains and separate bath-rooms. She'd never seen segregation like that, had you, Margo?"

"Sucked," Margo says. "But I loved that old hound dog of your daddy's."

"Dizzy," Margo says.

"And your mama showed me how to pick cotton."

"Don't you just love the good old days?" Ellen says icily. "Did you talk about what happened with Zoe, Margo? You were supposed to."

"We didn't talk at all," Sarah says. "Margo fell asleep the moment she hit the bed. It was wonderful lying next to her, hearing her breathe. We said our peace in our own quiet way, didn't we, Margo?"

Margo's face is pale. She glances nervously at Ellen "I didn't fall asleep."

"Dead to the world." Sarah puts some Bach fugues on the CD player. I'm feeling kind of bad. I have not made *my* peace with Margo, and I'm starting to wonder if I can take time off from work to take another trip East in September or October, to see Margo one last time. It would be so much easier leaving tomorrow knowing I'll see her again.

"Tell us more about that woman yesterday, Margo," Lana says, "after the grocery shopping." They had stopped to say hello to an old friend of Margo's, *not* an ex, who had recently moved from Manhattan to a bungalow in Sag Harbor.

"That woman doesn't know how to be intimate with people," Ellen growls.

"I thought she was delightful," Sarah says, pouring some wine.

"Plus, she's getting fat and wrinkled and old," Ellen says.

"She is old," Margo whispers. "She's worked hard and she'd created a good life for herself in Sag Harbor. Made new friends, swims every day and joined a book club."

"Everyone's in a book club these days," Ellen sighs. "Such a cliché."

"Manhattan's hard when you're older, Ellen. Hats off to her for starting a new life here. I'd buy a house in Sag Harbor if we could afford it. To be near the water. To be near Oyster Bay, where I..." She trails off, wiping an eye.

Ellen puts down a fork full of veggies. "You always defend your friends, Margo, and attack me."

Margo reddens. "How did I attack you?"

"You defend your friends and negate me. And they're all misfits."

Uh oh, I think, glancing at Margo.

"I resemble that remark," Sarah says affably, not taking the bait. "Anyone who *fits* in today's world is dangerous."

"Bet you a million dollars, Sarah, that Margo doesn't really love that woman's stuffy, cat-filled cottage," Ellen snorts.

Margo shrugs. "That woman, as you refer to her, owns an original vinyl album of Rosa Ponselle singing *'La forze del destino.'* I could have kissed her for that. Do you know how *rare* that album is?"

"What about the dungeon in her basement?" Ellen snorts.

"Oh, stop it." Margo sets the dachshund of the floor.

"What dungeon?" Lana asks.

Ellen shakes her head. "While you high-brows were talking opera, I took a look at those stockades and the S-M torture racks in her basement."

"Jesus, Ellen," Margo reddens. "Those were the gay guy's she bought the house from." She hobbles to the couch. "She'll take them out when she has the money to remodel. Anyway, what do you know about S-M? You wouldn't know a bullwhip from a cat-o-nine-trails."

"Jill knows a lot," Ellen says, leaning back in her chair and grinning at me.

"I do?" I sit up. It suddenly feels about one hundred degrees in this house.

Ellen laughs. "Tell them. Jill, about that friend of yours in California who has a slave she burns with cigarettes."

"She wasn't *my* friend," I say. "Vanessa knew her."

Sarah stares at me. "Did *you* torture someone, Jill?"

"I couldn't get out of that house fast enough."

Margo's laugh turns to a cough, which she can't seem to stop. We hold our collective breath. Betty brings her a glass of water. "But you went," she begins hoarsely, "to their sex show in the Tenderloin. You told me."

"That was years ago."

Ellen moves closer to me. "Vanessa's friend make some fat guy pull down his pants so she could whip him."

"These are your friends, Jill?" Lana strokes Betty's silky hair.

I shake my head. "An ex- of mine decided it would help her writing if we saw what an S-M slave relationship is like."

"Dear God," Sarah laughs. "Were you writing about sex slaves?"

"No, but Vanessa was convinced that by acting out past abuses she could heal herself from old hurts. Make them bearable, even pleasurable."

Sarah groans. "I think not."

"There are rules and code words," Betty pipes up from the end of the table, running her hands through her stylish purple hair. "If something doesn't feel right, you say a code word and your top or your bottom stops right away."

Everyone stares at Betty. These are some the first words she has spoken all day.

"Why can't you just say 'stop'?" Lana sits up.

"Because 'Stop' may be too close to the scene you're acting out," Betty says, getting into it. "So you use phrases that are unrelated to the role play."

"Have you done it?" Lana asks. "It would make a good first-person story for the magazine."

"No," Betty says. "I have clients who tell me things."

"What kind of code words do they use? Give me an example." Lana looks at Betty with interest.

"Like, I don't know, 'popcorn.'"

"Popcorn?" Margo laughs. It is wonderful to hear her laugh. We wait anxiously lest it become a cough, and when she laughs again, the present seems bearable. "Can't you hear it now? Vanessa's about to whip Jill with a cat o' nine tails, and she shouts, 'Popcorn!'"

Everyone laughs except me.

Sarah moves to the couch next to Margo. "We had romance in our day, didn't we, my friend? Candlelight dinners reading Rilke to each other. You sent me red roses with a line from *Der Rosenvalier*. I still have the card. '*I feel as if I've known you in another time and place.*' That was love, not cruelty masquerading as affection."

Ellen bolts to her feet. "Give me a break, Sarah." She starts to the kitchen, then turns, her eyes narrowing, hands becoming fists. "I am so bloody sick of all of your romantic fantasies about Margo." She pounds the dining-room table hard, spilling a glass of red wine. I plunge a paper napkin into the mess and begin to wipe. "If you really thought life was so much more wonderful in the past, you must have amnesia, Sarah. Have you forgotten that *you* broke up with Margo to go off with that professor at Brandeis?"

Sarah's eyes widen. "Actually, Ellen, Margo dumped me for Deena."

"Don't get me started on Deena," Ellen hisses.

"Poor Deena," Margo cries softly. "Alone on the floor of her kitchen for two days before Delores found her."

"Dear, sweet Deena," Ellen snorts. "Thank God I don't have to deal with *her* anymore."

"Stop it, Ellen!" Margo yells, trying to stand up, then sitting back down.

Ellen throws a glass into the sink. "The problem with you, Margo," she shouts, "with all of you, as a matter of fact, is that you're so busy rewriting the past you've forgotten what really happened." Ellen begins to towel up the mess she's made in the sink, then stops. "Margo doesn't adore any of you. She finds you…"

"Ellen!" Margo warns.

"You hate them, Margo. Admit it."

"I don't hate them," Margo cries. "What are you talking about?"

Ellen is pacing the room, a rabid dog about to sink her teeth. "Your friends think you love them."

"I do love them, Ellen. I —"

"And while you're denying it, tell them what *our* life is like," Ellen snorts, breathing fire over Margo's head. "Tell them how we had to refinance the house so we can pay the bills and how you can barely afford train fare to New York to drop off your portfolio with art directors, who won't even see you in person and probably don't open your samples because you're too old and too sick to waste their time? Have you told them?"

"Ellen, stop!" I yell. "We know you've struggled and that Margo hasn't had much freelance. But she makes enough to support you so you can write book after unpublishable book."

"Fuck you!" Ellen raises a fist in my face.

"Ellen! Jill! Stop it!" Sarah clears her throat, speaking quietly in her Southern drawl. "It's time for bed. It's been a long day. We can rehash the past and declare a victor in the morning."

"I want to talk now," Ellen screams, hitting the counter with her hand.

Sarah sighs. "I'll write you a check tonight if you're short."

"*Noblesse oblige*," Ellen hisses.

"Jesus, Ellen." Margo, wheezing, her face red, rises off the couch, turning to Sarah. "Thank you, Sarah. But we're OK. Ellen's exaggerating. She is right about one thing. I've got plenty of faults, and she knows them all."

"Oh, for fuck's sake, Margo." I shake my head. "We all have faults."

"Ellen takes very good care of me," Margo whispers.

"She's done an amazing job," I say. "But —"

"Damn right, I have," Ellen says, dropping next to Margo on the couch.

"And we all appreciate that," Lana offers.

"You don't give a rat's ass." Ellen slams down another glass. "You tolerate me so you can see Margo. I know how it works. I know what you think of me and my unpublishable books." She glares at me, then turns to Betty. "Some of you haven't spoken to Margo in years, and now you've come out of the woodwork because she's dying."

"Ellen, please," Margo says. "Let's go to bed." Six months ago, she would have insisted she was going to beat the cancer. That was before it went to her brain.

"Some of us haven't visited because you wouldn't let us," Betty cries, wiping her eyes.

"Bullshit!" Ellen screams. "Our house is a revolving door. You people come and go like maggots. I'm exhausted from making your meals and changing your sheets and taking you to the train so you can laugh and talk and enjoy Margo's last days on earth. But where were you, Betty, when I had to drive Margo to New York to see the oncologist? Have you counted out seven different medications eight times a day for her? That's not as much fun, is it? Where were you all when *I* was in the hospital?"

"You were in the hospital?" Lana says, dropping Betty's hand. "When?"

"None of you sent *me* flowers. Sarah didn't send me a thousand dollars so I could spend the day at Elizabeth Arden."

"You were only in the ER one night, sweetheart," Margo says quietly.

"When I called, you said you were fine," Sarah sighs, shaking her head.

Ellen's voice cracks. "That's not the point."

"What is the point?" Margo rubs her eyes.

"The point is, I'm giving up my life to take care of you, Margo. I haven't written a word in months or had a free day in two years. But your friends don't care about that. It's all about you, Margo. Wonderful, saintly Margo." She picks up a plastic paperweight, the Empire State Building in a snowstorm, and throws it on the kitchen floor, where it explodes. The dogs glance nervously at Margo as the rest of us scramble to clean up the globs of water and fake plastic snow.

"I care about you, Ellen," Margo wheezes, trying again to stand.

"Look what you're doing to me." Sobbing, Ellen pushes Margo down on the couch. Margo manages to pull herself up, stumbling out of the room and disappearing down the hall.

Ellen is doing it again, I think. *She wrecked last night with her seance and asthma attack, and she's determined to turn our last night with Margo into "Who's Afraid of Virginia Woolf?" Hump the hostess and get the guests, with Ellen in the starring role.*

Margo shuffles back into the room, holding a box of Kleenex in front of Ellen. "Here, hun. Don't cry."

Ellen looks up, grabs the box and throws it against the wall. The dogs jump. "Fuck you!"

Margo recoils.

"Why did you leave the room?"

Margo stokes the dog's head. "To bring you a Kleenex."

"You left me alone." Ellen shakes furiously. "Don't you understand? I don't want a Kleenex. I want you next to me, holding me. When you left the room I felt abandoned."

Oh my God, I think. *In their tiny, cloistered, merged universe, leaving the room for a Kleenex constitutes abandonment.*

"Why did you leave me?" Ellen demands.

Sarah stands up, clearing her throat. "Ellen, go to bed. The two of you need rest. We'll clean up in the morning."

"This is what real relationships are like, Sarah," Ellen shouts. "They're not sweet Southern delusions." She turns. "Are they, Margo?"

Margo, defeated, rubs a shaking hand across the remaining white stubble of hair on her head, her ears too big for her skull, her cheeks sunken and colorless.

"Tell everyone why you left the room, Margo," Ellen orders.

"You were crying. I thought…"

"That's not it!" Ellen shouts. "Tell them! You know."

I look at Margo, a woman defeated, the best friend I've ever had, allowing her partner to eviscerate her. Perhaps cancer is her only escape.

"I was afraid," she whispers.

"That's right, Margo. You were afraid because you were uncomfortable with my feelings."

We're all afraid of your feelings.

"What should I have done, Ellen?" Margo asks meekly. *Who is this woman? This strong, capable, generous woman I thought I knew.*

"I'll tell you what you should have done." Ellen inhales. Her asthma appears to have receded for the moment. "You should have held me in your arms and told me you love me. Anything but walk out of the room and leave me alone with your fucking exes glaring at me as if I'm a vampire." Ellen shakes her head. "I need to *feel* your love, Margo. I need you to show your friends how much you love me."

Wobbly, as if she being punished by the meanest nun in her grade school, Margo lowers herself onto her knees, reaching for Jill's hand. "I love you, Jill. More than life itself. I'm sorry I let you down."

This can't be happening.

"I love you, too," Ellen says, kissing Margo's head. "But why is it always up to me to tell the truth? Why am I the only one who's honest here? Why don't *you* tell them the truth once in a while?"

"We don't all have your courage, hun," Margo gasps.

"Courage to say what?" I ask. "Is there something we should know, Margo? Is there something you need to say to us?"

Sarah rises. "I think we've all said enough. I'm going to bed."

I swallow. *Say it. Say it.* "It's hard to be honest with you, Ellen, when you're firing at us at point blank range."

Ellen glares at me, flushed, eyes narrowed. "You're such a coward, Jill. When the going gets tough, you expect Margo to pick up the pieces. All the years we've listened to your fuck-ups and your idiotic relationships. All the years we've held your hand through your disasters with Vanessa and Pip and Sylvie, and you say I'm firing at you point blank. You're the one with the gun, Jill. You've been aiming at me since Margo and I met."

"Jesus," I say. The room is dead quiet. I can feel my heart banging in my chest as I walk toward the bedrooms. "Sarah's right. It's time for bed."

"Are you going to defend me, Margo?" Ellen's eyes are bright. "Or are you going to be nicer to your friends than you are to me?"

Margo, mouth open, looks hopelessly at Ellen. "I'm sorry you've had to take care of me, hun. And I'm sorry that my cancer means you're the one who gets left. It's not fair. I appreciate all your sacrifices. Can you forgive me?"

What is going on here? Margo has supported Ellen, used her publishing connections to get Jill's books published. Until she got sick, Margo did the shopping, cooked every meal, took care of Ellen when she was too weak from asthma or whatever to move. What more does Ellen want?

"Is that all you can say? 'I appreciate your sacrifices?'"

Is Ellen pure evil? She must hear my thoughts because her eyes lock on mine.

"I'll be relieved when Margo dies, Jill, because then I won't have to deal with you or any of Margo's other stupid exes. I won't have to try to be nice when I'm seething inside. It'll all be over, and Margo will be gone. And I'll be free." Ellen breathes her fire inches of my face. "I've fucking had it with you, Jill. Get out of this goddamned house."

I look at Sarah, then Margo, then the door. Where am I supposed to go? All of my stuff is here. We leave tomorrow. The candle on the coffee table flickers and a clock ticks in the kitchen.

"Get out, Jill!"

I start for the door and turn back to say goodbye to Margo.

Margo stands up. "Don't go, Jill."

Ellen glares at her. "Fuck you, Margo! Fuck both of you!" She hurls herself past me and out the front door. The rest of us sit in silence. After a moment, Margo lurches outside into the darkness. "Ellen!" she cries. "I love you. Come back!"

No one sleeps. In the morning we go our separate ways — me to California, Lana and Betty to Manhattan, Ellen and Margo to Hudson, Sarah to Boston.

In January, Ellen calls to say that Margo is dead.

Morgan and I fly east to the funeral. It is a bitter-cold day. Sarah, who has driven down from Boston, meets us at the motel in Hudson where all three of us stay.

In the morning, in a church filled with strangers, a white man in a gown reads the funeral liturgy, and Ellen, who has designed the service, lectures the audience on the precious sanctity of her marriage to Margo and the depth of their eternal love.

We don't know anyone at Ellen's brunch after the funeral. Lana and Betty were too upset by the ex-lovers' weekend to come. Deena is dead. Margo's friend from Sag Harbor and others from New York are too worn out by Ellen's volatile moods to say goodbye. We stand in the kitchen, in a crowd of strangers at their house, wondering what to do when Ellen spots us, asks us to remove our shoes, thanks us for coming, and moves on to greet other guests. After a few minutes, we drive to the Albany airport, and Morgan and I fly back to California.

———

This is the end, I think, as we take off. There is no ever-after. Margo is gone. Ellen is alive. She has the house to herself, and her dogs, and rooms full of rage.

WILD IRIS

Babies are wrecking us, Jill thinks, her heart kicking against her ribs as the telephone assaults them at four a.m. Morgan often gets calls from her apprentices or her business partner or laboring mothers at zero-dark-hundred, but this one is different.

"Your water broke?" Morgan is saying.

Jill swallows.

"But no contractions?"

Jill can tell from the warmth in Morgan's voice that she is talking to her daughter, Allie, who is not due for another month. Jill knows instantly that Morgan will be leaving this morning and be gone for weeks. She is a midwife, after all. Childbirth is her specialty. And this is her daughter.

"I'll find a flight and call you back," Morgan is saying. "I love you. Breathe. I'll be there soon." Morgan turns on the shower as she dials the airline. "We're having a baby, Jill. Want to come?"

"Can't," Jill says. "The special section's due next week."

Sixty minutes later, they are chasing the airport bus south down Highway 101 toward Mill Valley. Morgan, in the passenger seat, is on the phone to her business partner, brown leather backpack by her feet. Glenda, their red long-haired dachshund, is trembling in her lap.

Wizard, Glenda's black brother, also known as Mr. Wiz, lies curled in the backseat oblivious to the drama.

Halfway there, Morgan hands Jill a red envelope. "Happy Valentine's Day, sweetheart," she says.

"Happy Valentine's Day to you." Jill reaches for the heart-shaped box of See's candies she's hidden under a scarf in the back seat. Tomorrow is February Fourteenth.

"Ooooh," Morgan says, brushing a strand of her streaked blond mane from her eyes. "I'll try not to eat them all on the plane. Can you cancel our reservations for the Buckeye tomorrow night?"

"What about my birthday?" Jill says.

"Boo hoo," Morgan smiles sadly.

Jill tries to open Morgan's card with her teeth as she guides the Honda into the Airporter lot by Highway 101 in Mill Valley. The card is handmade, unexpectedly lacy, cut from a doily and decorated with sparkly red glitter and a heart-shaped photo of Morgan, Jill, and the dogs at Muir Beach.

"When'd you have time to make this?" Morgan barely has time to breathe these days, having opened a new midwifery office in Berkeley.

"At that birth last week in West Marin. The kids were making Valentines, and I joined them between contractions. Don't forget me." Morgan leans over to kiss her.

Jill, Glenda and the Wiz watch Morgan board the bus in the dewy light as kayakers and rowers slide across Richardson Bay to the east. Despite the raw cold in New Mexico, Morgan is dressed for springtime, in a straw hat, white linen pants, a beige pullover, and a silk scarf from Thailand. She looks terrific, her blue eyes alert and ready for action.

She waves to Jill as the bus driver scans the parking lot for stragglers, then whooshes the door closed. Forgotten on the seat next to Jill are the chocolates Morgan left in her rush to catch the bus. Jill glances at her watch: Six A.M. Too late to go back to sleep; she might as well hike with the dogs on the open space by the college near their house.

———

A light rain falls by the empty ball fields. Walking the dogs on the long retractable leashes is hard without Morgan because Glenda, always anxious, constantly stops to sniff and look behind her for her other human. And the Wiz, who hates rain, digs in his heels, only moving if Jill coaxes him with treats. Naturally, Jill has forgotten to bring treats. *I can win this war,* she tells herself, gazing up at oak-forested hills on the far side of the playing fields.

Crossing the wooden bridge over the creek, Jill feels a tightening in her chest and tears in her eyes. Morgan has been gone a lot lately, at births, taking care of her grandson, shopping for her mother in San Francisco, and flying as often as she can to New Mexico because Allie's pregnancy has been difficult.

Glenda howls so shrilly Jill's ears hurt. A woman with blond hair in a red felt hat, red down vest, and blue jeans overtakes them.

"That's quite a greeting," the woman laughs, crouching down so Glenda can sniff her hand. She pets the Wiz, who, as always, is wagging his tail.

"I'm headed straight up," Jill says to the woman, whom she thinks she and Morgan have passed several times on the trail. Jill cannot remember her name. "Want to walk with us?"

The woman assesses the hill ahead. "It's awfully steep."

"It'll make your heart pound, but you'll feel good after."

"Where's Morgan?"

"New Mexico," Jill says, surprised the woman knows Morgan's name. "I'm Jill, by the way."

"I know," laughs the woman. "We've met before. I'm Grace."

"I'm terrible at names."

"Why is Morgan in New Mexico?" Grace pushes up the brim of her red hat.

"Her daughter's water broke, and she flew off this morning to be with her."

"Exciting," Grace says.

"Very." Jill chews her lip. *I have more than enough love to go around,* Morgan often reassures. She might have enough love, Jill thinks, but she doesn't have enough time, especially when she's up all night at births and manages three offices and talks constantly to clients and to her midwifery partner and her apprentices and to her family. It doesn't seem quite fair because Jill doesn't have any family and has only one job to distract her.

"You have *my* family," Morgan often says. But Morgan's family doesn't feel the same as blood relatives.

"My daughter is way too obsessed with her Internet start-up to think about having kids," the woman Grace is saying, trying to catch her breath. "I wish she would have some babies."

"What is it about mothers and grandkids?" Jill asks. "My mother always wanted them. I thought she was lucky to have me, alive."

"Meaning? You don't like children? Or you almost died?" The woman's penetrating brown eyes study Jill, who is watching the rivulets of rainwater stream down the rutted grooves in the clay road.

"A new grandchild means Morgan will be busier and gone more."

"You miss her when she travels?"

Yes, Jill misses her. In the beginning she is happy to have more free time, but after a week or so, she gets lonely and then jealous and then angry. She's not proud of herself for feeling for this, but it's how she is. "Morgan says I'm self-centered."

The woman laughs. "Everyone's self-centered. It's the human condition." She stops to catch her breath. "Don't wait if I'm too slow." The Wiz has stopped directly in front of Grace to sniff some owl scat, his leash twisting around her legs. Glenda moves closer for a sniff, wrapping around Grace's other side. Jill tries to execute a complicated leash arabesque over Grace's shoulders, and as she does, notices that Grace smells pleasantly of green-apple soap.

Glenda charges forward as soon as she is liberated.

"I love the way she runs. When I master my new animation program, I'd like to draw her," Grace says.

"Glenda would love to be in a movie."

Grace smiles. "Likes to see her name in lights?"

"Something like that."

They have reached the crest of the hill that opens onto a grassy meadow, where tufts of high grass grow in clumps on both sides of the road. Then the trail sinks and turns and climbs again, narrowing as it enters a thicket of coast oaks. "Is learning animation hard?"

"Not as hard as it was in the old days," Grace says. "Come over and play with my software sometime."

Jill nods. "I'd like to." She knows she never will.

"I'm online way too much," Grace says. "I talk more to people in e-mails and texts than I do in person. You could be the only live human I speak to all week."

"Wow." Jill likes solitude but not that much.

The road narrows through the woods, zigzags to the left and loops back around and down the hill, where streams of water gurgle over the low spots. Wizard leaps over the puddles without Jill having to drag him. "They're being uncharacteristically cooperative," Jill says. "I think they like you."

The woods have that sweet, fresh smell, of rain and grass and leaves that have fallen from the madrones, coast oaks, and bay laurels. They pass the small pond, where a woman is tossing a stick for a golden retriever. Dogs aren't allowed to swim in the pond, and the rangers get mad if they catch them.

"Naughty, naughty," Grace laughs, watching the woman and dog.

At the car, Jill cradles Wiz in a towel as she sits on the back bumper, wiping dirt from his belly and paws.

"Hairy little beast," Grace says.

"Thanks for coming with us." Jill sets the Wiz on the back seat and dries Glenda.

"It was fun walking with you."

"We're here every morning," Jill says.

"Maybe tomorrow, then."

Morgan calls at nine that night. "Allie's been in labor nearly twenty-four hours, and she's only four centimeters. "She's... Whoa! Another contraction. Gotta go. Love you."

———

At six A.M the next day, the phone rings. "We have a baby girl," Morgan says. "She's a six-pound, one-ounce angel."

"Congratulations," Jill says. "What's her name?"

"Doesn't have one yet. I think they want their teacher to name her."

"How's Allie?"

"Had a C-section because her cervix never fully dilated. So she's very disappointed. And very sore."

"She's lucky to have you there," Jill says.

"Oops. Her father just arrived. Gotta go. Love you."

"I love you, too." But Morgan has hung up; she must be congratulating her ex-husband on their new grandchild.

It is raining lightly in the parking lot by the ball fields. Glenda, glaring accusingly at Jill for bringing her out in wet weather, lunges at the red Jetta that pulls up next to them, then wags her tail furiously.

"Hey," Grace smiles. She is wearing a red rain slicker and floppy hat.

"You're upbeat this morning," Jill says.

"Am I?" Grace slams the car door. "I guess I'm happy to see you. Happy to be out on this glorious wet morning. And happy because I solved a design problem." Glenda paws the ground, preparing to roll in coyote poop.

"No!" Jill yells, too late. Glenda has rolled.

Grace laughs. "I can take her."

"Great." Jill hands Grace the leash. Soon Glenda is prancing along beside Grace like a show dog. So is the Wiz.

"You've got magical powers over them."

Grace glances at Jill as they climb up the fire road. "What do you do?"

"What?"

"For a living."

"Work at a newspaper."

Grace eyes her curiously. "Are you a reporter?"

Jill nods.

"Have you seen a dead body?"

Jill laughs. "Not on the job."

Grace looks quizzical. "I thought reporters were always stumbling across dead bodies."

"I saw my mother dead," Jill says. "Our crime reporter sees a corpse sometimes, but not that often."

"Look." Grace points to the grass beyond the road. "Wild iris."

The flowers are cobalt against the green grass. The glorious deep blue makes Jill happy.

"All yesterday I was thinking about you," Grace says suddenly. "I wanted to know more about you and Morgan. It was so nice to talk to someone who wasn't on a computer."

"Talk away," Jill says. Grace looks kind of pretty this morning in her red hat and mass of dyed blond hair.

Jill meets Grace nearly every day as spring gushes up from the earth and down from the sky, bringing red warriors and wild monkey flowers and more yellow and purple iris.

"I've been walking every day with that woman Grace," Jill tells Morgan when she calls. "The dogs love her."

"Allie's cat has the runs," Morgan says. "I've spent the last two hours shampooing the carpets."

"Grace wants to adopt Glenda."

"Fantastic," Morgan laughs. "Sign the adoption papers before she changes her mind."

Jill sighs. Morgan has no idea that she has begun to feel a stir of attraction for Grace. Jill should tell her, just to dispel the weirdness. She and Morgan have vowed not to keep secrets from each other. On the other hand, if she tells Morgan she'd have to let go of the swoony, excited feeling in her legs and the fantasy of forbidden sex with a stranger. It's nothing serious, just a fantasy, so why alarm Morgan? Plus, it diverts Jill from Morgan's absence, and Morgan still doesn't know when she's coming home. It's got to be soon because Morgan can't find enough midwives to fill in for her. *No need to confess*, Jill tells herself, noting that she's started taking more time than usual picking which blue jeans, which baseball cap and which raincoat to wear on

her morning hikes with Grace. What does that mean? *Nothing*, she tells
herself.

"My husband died when our daughter was six months old," Grace
tells Jill that morning. Grace often shares long and complicated stories
that Jill enjoys. Jill wishes Morgan would tell long stories, with phys-
ical details and character development and as many digressions as she
likes, but Morgan says she runs out of things to say.

"My daughter graduated from U.C. Davis two years ago," Grace is
saying. "So he died a long time ago."

"What happened?"

"A motorcycle crash."

"Wow. I'm sorry."

"It took years to get over, but eventually I fell in love with Josh, and
we lived together for nine years, until he left me for someone younger.
My world crashed three years ago. I had a hysterectomy, lost my
company, lost Josh, had to sell my house in Sonoma County, and
moved here. I'm finally on stable footing. Coming out of hiding."

"What did your company do?"

"Designed and manufactured baby clothes. I still do that but for
another company, not my own."

Jill bites her lip. Babies again. They keep popping up in her life.

"You don't like babies, do you?" Grace stops on the steep hill to
look at her.

"I like them. But they take a lot of time."

Grace laughs. "Does Morgan's granddaughter have a name yet?"

Jill shakes her head. "Their teacher hasn't given her one."

"What kind of teacher?"

To change the subject, because Morgan doesn't like Jill talking
about the spiritual community Morgan had once been part of, Jill
describes the land she and Morgan have recently bought in the mountains of Mendocino County, where they plan to build a house and
maybe move one day.

"I hope you don't move soon," Grace frowns. "I'd miss you."

Heat jazzes Jill's legs as Grace squeezes her hand.

A morning later, a deer leaps across the path ahead of them; Wiz barks and yanks on his leash, desperate to chase it. Glenda chokes as she pulls.

"You know, where I lived in Sonoma County," Grace says, after the commotion is over, "our house bordered public open space, and deer used to hide from the sun under our deck. One day a buck went underneath the deck. We heard him down there for ages, bumping around, and then we heard nothing for a long time, and then the smell began. Josh finally went under and lugged out his carcass and laid him down by the stream below the house. After a few weeks, the buck was nothing but bones. The vultures and coyotes and bugs ate everything else. Josh turned his bones into a sculpture."

"The bones?" Jill says.

"He was very inventive."

Jill gives Wiz a treat for not pulling. "Something died once at our house, and we couldn't figure out where the stink was coming from until it got so awful we peered under the deck and spotted a raccoon carcass. He'd crawled in through a hole in the lattice. Morgan held my hand while I reached through the slats to pull him out by the tail. We were both afraid the raccoon might come back from the dead and bite us."

"I understand," Grace nods. "Raccoons are pesky. We used to feed the raccoons at our house. I enjoyed them so much I started feeding the squirrels. Did I tell you that story? Stop me if I did."

"Tell me," Jill says.

They turn right into the oak forest. "I fed the squirrels every day for two years."

"Two years?"

"They were so cute that sometimes I drew them on baby clothes. The squirrels had their babies, and their babies had babies, and on and on, and it didn't stop. Until..." She pauses ominously. "I learned my lesson."

"What was that?" Jill asks, taking off her rain hood as the sun emerges from behind a cloud.

"It's a long story."

"I love long stories." Jill also loves the funny purr in her legs she feels when Grace tells long stories. It makes Jill feel alive and happy, especially now that Morgan's phone conversations end so abruptly, with the baby crying or the eleventh load of laundry needing folding or Morgan's mother calling from San Francisco to say she can't get down the stairs to go to the market.

"After a while," Grace continues as they hike around the pond, where the coots and mallards swim and the woman with the golden retriever is throwing a stick for the dog. "I was feeding what seemed like hundreds of squirrels a day with peanuts and raw vegetables and cat kibble. They'd stand on their little back legs and beg at the kitchen door and deck windows. They were so cute. I was completely infatuated."

"Saint Francis of Assisi," Jill says.

"I was insane," Grace says. "But it didn't come to a head until Josh and I went to Hawaii for two weeks — our first vacation in years — and my daughter and her boyfriend came over from Davis to stay at the house. They decided they didn't want to feed all the squirrels, which I understand, but the squirrels got restless and hungry, and then they got angry. Really mad."

"Wow," Jill says, shaking her head. "How do you know when a squirrel is mad?"

"It was summer, and they chewed through the screen doors when my daughter was at work, broke into the house and rooted through the kitchen and pantry and every conceivable drawer they could open. They had these horrible battles over the food, or lack of food, and one squirrel got mauled to death. My daughter found his carcass and blood all over the kitchen."

"My God." Jill stops. Grace stops, too.

"I was still in Hawaii, and my daughter didn't tell me what was going on because she didn't want to spoil our vacation, but the squirrels drove her and her boyfriend nuts. When I came home and saw the damage, I realized how foolish I'd been, and I resolved never to feed wild animals again."

Grace's weird story has warmed every part of Jill's body. She doesn't know why exactly. Morgan prefers TV when she gets home to recapping childbirth tales from births she's just attended. Mostly, she says, her job is like a pilot's — exciting take-offs and landings with a lot of boring down time in between.

"Am I boring you?" Grace's brown eyes brighten curiously,

"I'm riveted. Is there more?"

"There is a little more." Grace gives Glenda one of the special treats she's started bringing for the dogs as they continue down the hill. "That horrible squirrel invasion was the beginning of my daughter's weird squirrel karma. Squirrel things kept happening to her. At Christmas, I always have a holiday tree and make ornaments and string lights, which can take me days, because I'm obsessive. I love doing it. I don't know why, but I made this squirrel ornament even though my daughter was still angry about what happened with the squirrels."

"Angry at you?" Jill asked.

"At the squirrels. And to take revenge, she glued a jalapeño pepper on the squirrel-ornament's crotch. We all thought it was funny because it looked like a penis. But soon after that, back at college, a squirrel leaped on her from the trees for no reason whatsoever and bit her so hard she had to get stitches and a tetanus shot. The next thing I knew, my daughter won a grant to study squirrels in South America."

"Seriously?" Even Glenda seems to be listening. "After all that trauma she wanted to study squirrels?"

"Yes," Grace nods. "She became a zoologist. Right after she returned from her trip to Brazil, she began to feel really sick. By the time we got her to the hospital, she was in a coma and stayed in a coma for a week. We were afraid she would die. The doctors said she might not come out of it. I was terrified. But she got well."

"What made her so sick?"

"Spinal meningitis."

"Oh, no." Jill looks into the sky thinking of her mother's friend Labelle, who'd died of meningitis years ago in Philadelphia.

Grace touches Jill's arm. "The whacky thing is that while we were in the emergency room waiting to find out what was wrong with my daughter, Josh and I looked up on the TV, and there was this skinned squirrel pinned to the side of a log cabin."

"Strange," Jill shivers.

"I told my daughter when she recovered that she had bad squirrel karma because she glued the plastic penis on the squirrel ornament."

"Sounds like you both had bad squirrel karma," Jill offers.

"You're right," Grace sighs. "But hers was worse. I wish you could have seen all those squirrels staring at us, begging for food. Sometimes we were afraid to go out."

"Sounds like a scene from *The Birds*."

"I should write a script," Grace nods.

They were back at the parking lot.

"Tomorrow's my birthday," Jill says suddenly. It is only raining lightly.

Grace looks surprised. "Can I make you a birthday breakfast after our walk tomorrow?"

Jill hesitates. "Tomorrow's Saturday."

"Is that a problem?"

"It's good, actually. I don't go to work."

"Good. I'll see you tomorrow then, around nine?"

"No squirrels at your house?" Jill opens the car door for the dogs.

Grace laughs. "Nope. That door is closed. No more squirrels."

The next morning, Morgan calls. "Happy Birthday, Jill!"

"I wish you were here."

"Are you having a party?"

"Grace is making me a breakfast."

"Have fun," Morgan says. Jill can hear the baby gurgling on her shoulder. "Allie's sleeping. The little one kept her up all night. Uh oh. She's awake. Needs breakfast. Gotta go. Can't wait to see you."

"Do you have a date yet?"

"Maybe next week. Or the week after. Allie still needs help. It takes a while to get on your feet after a C-section."

"Hurry," Jill says.

"Whoops, there's the doorbell. Have fun."

———

Jill should have told Morgan that she didn't trust herself to be alone with Grace, that all their walking and talking with the dogs amid the wild iris and red warrior flowers and gurgling streams have stirred some fever inside her. Something about Grace's weird stories and her artist's eye and her eagerness to get to know Jill had aroused her. Jill knows she is on dangerous ground. She's been here before, but nothing has happened. And if something does happen, maybe it's time she and Morgan consider non-monogamy, or polyamory, or serial monogamy, or whatever they're calling extra-marital sex these days. Because if Morgan is always busy, Jill should be allowed some fun, shouldn't she? And this flirtation-light with Grace is harmless. Grace is casual and breezy, not interested in a real relationship. On the other hand, she isn't racing off to take care of children or grandchildren and other people's babies bursting out. Grace is actually much more like Jill than Morgan, with her love of stories and her artistic temperament. Anyway, nothing is going to happen. Jill will have breakfast and come home.

So that is that. Jill will not tell Morgan about her attraction to Grace, just have breakfast with her because it is her birthday. Jill will give herself the gift of that swirly, dizzy, floaty feeling, then go home. She won't have to confess anything because this attraction is all in her mind. Everyone's life would be a continuous confession if their fantasies required an admission of guilt.

In the morning, Jill feels so tense dressing for her hike with Grace that she swallows the last Valium a doctor prescribed several years ago for neck spasms. By the time they meet in the parking lot by the college, the little black and green pill has made its way into Jill's bloodstream, causing her tongue to stick slightly to her mouth, her heart to thud happily in her chest, and her nerves to loosen like clothes on a line in a summer breeze. She is happy and guilt-free, ready for whatever happens. *Happy Birthday, Jill,* she says to herself.

"Hey," Grace smiles from her red Jetta. "Happy Birthday."

"Hey." Jill feels light-headed and excited.

As they walk up the fire road, Grace fills the silence with a story about her niece, who has a case of something Grace calls "punctuation weirdness," capitalizing all common nouns and putting semicolons where commas should go. Morgan would never tell Jill a punctuation story. Morgan hasn't a clue where a semicolon goes.

Jill stops fighting the pleasant effect of Grace's words have on her body as they walk side by side, enjoying the not-knowing what will happen next. At the parking lot by the ball fields, Jill and the dogs follow Grace's red car to her townhouse in the woods nearby. The dogs will stay in Jill's car because it is still cool in the shade, and Grace has cats.

"Scrambled eggs, bacon and waffles," Grace says placing the plates on the circular oak table in her kitchen. "And fresh-squeezed OJ. And, later, a birthday surprise."

"Wow," Jill says. Grace looks inviting in her tight red T-shirt. She has never seen Grace with her raincoat off.

As they eat, Grace gazes meaningfully into Jill's eyes. For some reason, Jill tells Grace about the time her mother placed her and her sister in an iron lung on display at the Vermont State Fair.

"Why?" Grace seems startled.

"We were fascinated by this long silver cylinder with a real woman's head poking out. Polio was rampant, remember, and they had an empty iron lung, and we wanted to try it out. My mother laid us right down inside it."

"How 'bout we lay down upstairs?" Grace says, placing their plates in the sink.

Lie down, Jill corrects in her head. "Are you sleepy?"

"Not sleepy," Grace says. "Ready for some fun."

"OK," Jill gulps, wondering if this is a good idea.

Grace takes her hand, leading her upstairs to a bedroom with a king-sized bed and walls painted purple, with purple curtains and sheets and a white down quilt. Grace falls on the mattress, pulling Jill on top of her; out of nowhere, three cats appear, staring at them from various positions around the room.

"Does it matter that we don't know each other that well?" Jill asks, feeling odd. She hopes the Valium is not wearing off.

"How well do we need to know each other?" Grace's knee presses between Jill's legs. "We've been getting to know each for weeks. I'm ready, sweetheart. More than ready. Don't you want to? You know you do." As she kisses Jill, her aromatic mint saliva accumulates in Jill's mouth.

"Jees," Jill says. "I'm... you're..."

"What?" Grace places a hand on Jill's breast.

For some reason, Jill is thinking of Morgan's tiny new grand-daughter in Santa Fe.

"Come on," Grace says, her brown eyes glittering. "Play with me. I know you want to."

"I do," Jill swallows. "I've been wondering for some time what you'd feel like."

"This is what I feel like." Grace is pulling off her red T-shirt and her bra. Her full white breasts shimmer in the morning sun, and the ying-yang tattoo on her left bicep make Jill's insides swirl and her crotch sticky. Grace slides herself against Jill's knees, and they are a hot, writhing tangle until Grace reaches down, pulling something out of a paper bag.

"Look!" Grace cries.

For a minute, Jill's afraid it is a live squirrel or raccoon, but no, she is holding a long green vegetable, a Japanese cucumber or a zucchini.

"Cool," Jill says, trying to sit up.

"Stay down, sweetheart," Grace orders. "It's organic. From Whole Foods."

Jill gulps. Grace is putting a zucchini inside her.

"You beautiful woman." Grace slides the zucchini deeper, begin-ning to move it in and out.

"I'm not sure there's room for it," Jill says.

"Oh, there's room for it." Grace presses harder, completely on top of Jill now and grinding against her. "I've never made love to a woman before, and I love it. I love it."

Jill hadn't realized how extremely turned on she is, how ready she is for this, how hot this feeling is of Grace's breasts smooshing against hers and her big, fat zucchini rippling inside.

"Come on, Jill," Grace yells. "Let me have you, you gorgeous woman!" Grace is riding her, howling in a way that starts her cats howling, too. Jill howls along with them as Grace envelopes her, reaching for something else beside the bed. "Here," she says, handing Jill an even bigger zucchini and lifting her hips so Jill can insert it. "This one's for me. Quick, you delicious monkey."

A calico cat leaps onto the bed, sticking his whiskers in Jill's face. Grace meows her feline joy. "Deeper, Jill. Deeper. Don't stop. I love this. I love the feel of you inside me." Grace is writhing, at first on top and then under her. "I'm keeping you here forever," she moans. "I need this. I need you." Her eyes are so bright and savage Jill has to look at the purple curtains for relief. "I surrender, Jill. I surrender." Letting out a long, ecstatic wail, Grace contracts, moans and collapses. The giant cucumber slips out of her.

"Did you come?" Grace is beginning to catch her breath.

Jill laughs. "I'm not sure if I came or the cucumber did."

"Let's do it again," Grace cries, grabbing her robe from a chair and heading downstairs. "I've got a carrot and an *aubergine* in the vegetable drawer."

"An eggplant?" Jill says. "I hope it's Japanese." She isn't sure she can accommodate a parmigiana-sized eggplant.

"It's a beauty. A nice big purple one," Grace calls. "I'm not letting you go until Morgan comes home. When is that exactly?"

The thought of being held captive with Grace until Morgan comes home alarms Jill, who wipes herself on the sheet, pulls on her clothes, tiptoes down the stairs and slips out the back door as Grace tosses vegetables from the fridge into a carry-on bag.

Glenda and the Wiz dance as Morgan steps out of the airport bus.

"How's the baby?" Jill says. "Does she have a name? How's Allie?"

"I missed you horribly," Morgan says, kissing Jill's cheek. "They're both doing great. No name yet. Did you finish your special section? How's Grace? What did she make for your birthday breakfast?"

Me, Jill almost blurts. "A zucchini dish." Jill pulls out of the parking lot.

"She has a crush on you, I think." Morgan scratches the Wiz, holding Glenda close. "Do you have a crush on her?"

"For twenty minutes, but it's over," Jill says, almost driving off Highway 101. "She's crazy."

"I knew that when you told me about her squirrels."

"But she's genius with zucchinis."

"Cool," Morgan says. "Make me the dish, OK? I'm so tired of cooking."

"For sure," Jill smiles, winking at the dogs and handing Morgan the box of chocolates she left behind a month ago. "Happy Valentine's Day."

THE OTHERS ARE GOLD

The day after Christmas is cold, and Highway 101, usually crammed with cars, is empty this early in the morning. The flanking pastures are green and dotted with black and white cows. Jill stops to use the restroom at McDonald's in Petaluma, where a group of young men are reading the Bible, and a mother in a red Santa hat, with kids dressed in elf pajamas, is devouring Sausage McMuffins.

"Jingle Bell Rock" blares from the speakers as Jill glances at herself in the bathroom mirror. Her white hair is cropped short and her clothes — down jacket, turtleneck and jeans — are black.

Driving down from Mendocino County, Jill has replayed dozens of scenes with Vanessa, with whom she'd fallen in love decades ago, believing, at the time, that chemistry is destiny, and a sexual attraction as strong as theirs had to be pursued. And so, with trepidation, desperate with desire, Jill had left her comfortable life with Margo to join Vanessa's mountainside household in Marin — three dogs, seven cats and her boyfriend Dean, whom Vanessa insisted was gay.

"It's the most wonderful time the year," Andy Williams sings. *So wonderful,* Jill thinks, *that the star of "The Apprentice" is the U.S. President, and Lana is locked in a dementia unit, and Margo is dead. And Ellen, Margo's widow, is fit as a fiddle, promoting her memoir about Margo's last days on earth.*

With Margo's help, Jill escaped Vanessa.

Back in the car, Jill types an address in Google Maps. A woman's voice directs her through downtown Petaluma. Jill tries to remember when she last saw Vanessa. Probably at their women's group reunion, years ago, when Jill and Vanessa had led a ritual together. At the end, Jill suggested the group sing a song from her childhood:

Make new friends
And keep the old
Some are silver
And the others are gold.

Jill parks her car, holding her breath as she enters a low brick building, where a blue-and-white Christmas tree blinks by the door, and a dazed man in a wheelchair stares into space. A young woman in scrubs gives Jill a visitor's badge, leading her down the hallway. *All I want for Christmas is you,* Mariah Carey croons from somewhere.

The three beds in the room are empty. Jill looks at her watch. She is fifteen minutes early. Three others from the long-ago women's group will be here soon. So will Vanessa's daughter, Valerie. The last time Jill saw her, Valerie was a girl in her junior-high-school soccer uniform attending a fundraiser with her mother at a homeless shelter in Marin. Valerie is thirty years old now. Her father, the ship's captain, died years ago. *Was it cirrhosis. A stroke? Maybe both.* Someone had said Vanessa and Valerie discovered him dead on the floor of his apartment. When was that exactly? Jill and the sea captain never liked each other.

A movement catches Jill's eye as she stands in the doorway. There, she sees suddenly, in the middle bed, lies a person, tiny and still, buried beneath the sheets, curled in the fetal position.

Jill swallows, stepping closer, heart pounding. "Hello?"

The tiny being does not respond.

"Are you awake?" Jill whispers. It looks more like E.T., from the movie, than a person. A bandage is taped above the right eye.

"Hey, there!" A young woman enters, blond hair pulled back in a ponytail. She is wearing a Vassar College sweatshirt and black yoga pants. She could be Vanessa thirty years ago. But this is Valerie, Vanessa's daughter, with her mother's bright eyes and radiant smile, but much taller and more athletic.

"Thanks for coming." Valerie says, kneeling next to the bed. "Mama," she says, kissing the wrinkled cheek. "You have a visitor. Do you see her? Can you open your eyes?"

Vanessa? Yes, this is Vanessa.

Jill remembers suddenly a hallucination she had thirty-five years ago, when she and Vanessa took LSD. Before Jill's eyes, Vanessa changed from a young woman to a crone to a skeleton. Terrified, Jill had driven, stoned out of her mind, to San Francisco to find Margo.

"Mama," Valerie is saying as she touches Vanessa's shoulder and checks her bandage. "Your cut looks better today."

"Did she fall?" Jill asks quietly.

"Getting out of bed." Valerie pulls up a chair. "Sit down, Jill, where you can see each other."

Jill sits, thinking of Morgan at home, lacing up her hiking boots as she and Morgan's daughter and her daughter's boyfriend prepare to walk in the hills.

"Mama," Valerie repeats, tapping Vanessa's hand.

Vanessa opens her eyes, the same stunning brown eyes as Valerie's but streaked with yellow now.

She can't hurt me, Jill tells herself. *She cannot draw me back into her web.*

"Mama. Can you say good morning to Jill?" Valerie is so patient and loving. Does she bear her mother any ill will for her strange, unconventional childhood and Vanessa's changing cast of male and female lovers?

"Jill's driven down from Mendocino to visit you, Mama," Valerie says, studying her mother's chart. "Ginny and Celine and Jackie are coming, too."

Vanessa makes a snuffling noise as she breathes, a kind of gurgle. She opens her eyes and stares at Jill, giving no sign of recognition. Her skin is paper thin, exhausted and bruised. Jill's throat constricts.

"Mama's been sleeping a lot," Valerie is saying. "The new meds help the agitation but make her sleepy." Valerie kisses her mother's head, stroking her gray hair with gentle fingers. "Open your eyes, Mama?" Valerie taps her shoulder. "Wake up!" Jill half hopes Vanessa will *not* wake up. If she does, perhaps she will be angry at Jill for running away in the night three decades ago.

"Mama," Valerie calls from across the divide. But Mama's eyes don't open. There is no smile on her lips. "Let's get her up." Valerie pulls down the covers. Her mother is fully dressed in a navy sweatshirt, black tights, and yellow sneakers.

Three friends now stand in the doorway.

"Merry Christmas, Vanessa," cries Ginny, the minister who started their women's group years ago. She wears a bright-yellow down vest; her white hair is cut neatly at her shoulders; her blue eyes are clear and discerning. "How wonderful to see you."

Celine, whose parents owned racehorses, wears a green sweater and green slacks and green shoes. Jackie, now the top seller at her real estate agency, who once bewitched Jill with her Texas drawl and sensual lips, wears eye makeup and frosted hair and a nervous smile. They all kiss Vanessa's cheek.

Vanessa, disconcerted by the commotion around her, mumbles something incomprehensible to her daughter.

All of us are crones now, Jill thinks. *Much closer to death than birth. But, at least we're not wasting in the borderlands, where Vanessa has somehow parked herself.*

With everyone there, Valerie brings her mother to the edge of the bed, lifting her, asking Ginny and Celine to take an arm and help Vanessa down the hall.

"Good for you, Mama," Valerie cheers. "You're up and walking."

All six of them pass slowly down the linoleum hallway to the front door, setting off an alarm. Valerie waves to the woman at the check point, who presses something electronic to open the door.

Jill feels tight and cold walking in the parking lot behind Ginny and

Celine and Vanessa, who is bent over, her back parallel to the ground, like a gnome.

"Wow," Jackie says to Jill, who is next to her. "Did the surgery do this?"

"I'm not sure." Jill inhales. "Someone, Ginny, I think, said the operation took thirteen hours, and she was unconscious for three weeks after and hasn't been the same since. I don't know the details. I haven't seen Vanessa in years."

"She was such a goddess," Jackie sighs.

Jill nods.

"And so smart," Jackie continues.

"Irresistible," Jill muses.

"To you, maybe," Jackie sighs. "Must have been some horrible surgery." She touches Jill's hand. "I'll never forget that Summer Solstice ritual when she invoked the goddess and insisted we all walk naked down to her swimming pool, which she'd filled with flowers."

"And we all jumped in," Jill laughs.

"You did," Jackie winks. "Big time."

Valerie leads Vanessa back inside and along the linoleum floor, the others following. The staff have found a place where they can visit with Vanessa while she eats her lunch. Among treadmills and ellipticals, they take turns feeding Vanessa from a plate of brown meat and watery vegetables. Everyone is laughing, but their faces are strained. They are not really having fun. No one is having fun. Vanessa is bent forward, half dead, not having fun, not speaking.

Jill steps back, taking a photo of the group with her phone. She wants to be able to remember this scene. She wants to show Morgan what Vanessa has become.

"Well done, Mama," Valerie says kindly. "You've eaten all your lunch and had a walk with your friends."

"S'riahsh," Vanessa says, eyes fixed on Valerie.

"What did she say?" Ginny asks.

"She wants to go back to bed," Valerie says. "Don't you, Mama?"

Vanessa's head nearly drops in her plate.

Ginny and Celine and Jackie get up quickly.

"I'll take her from here," Valerie says, guiding Vanessa down the hall. "Thank you all for coming."

"Can we take you to lunch?" Jill asks. "We have so many questions. We're counting on it."

Valerie checks her phone. "I'd love to, but I have to be at work in fifteen minutes."

"Where do you work?" Jackie asks brightly.

"At a nursing home."

"Wow," Jill says.

They take turns kissing Vanessa's pale cheek.

"Goodbye, Vanessa." Jill leans over the bed.

Without warning, Vanessa sits up and opens her eyes. "You!" she blurts, clear as a bell, pointing a trembling finger at Jill, then dropping back to the fetal position.

They eat at an inn where Ginny has made reservations. Everyone is in shock.

"Valerie is a wonderful nurse," Jackie says, wiping away tears.

"And wonderful daughter," Celine nods.

Ginny takes a bite of her hamburger. "She turned down a full scholarship to law school to care of Vanessa."

"How long has Vanessa been so..." Jackie stops.

"Four years, I think," Ginny says. "She couldn't live by herself after the operation, and she didn't have a home because she gave her house to the man she was living with at the time. So Valerie moved with Vanessa into a tiny studio and has taken care of her ever since. They don't have a penny. Valerie's father was destitute when he died. "

"Terrible," says Celine, who is an heiress.

"It's..." Jill shakes her head. "Unbelievable."

"She remembered you though, Jill," Jackie says, eyes wide.

Valerie carries Vanessa's ashes in a small wooden box.

They make an altar for her mother on the sand at Limantour Beach on Point Reyes, Vanessa's favorite place. On a turquoise lungi, they place photos of Vanessa and Valerie and the sea captain, and Vanessa and Jill, and Vanessa and her mother. Valerie brings a ruby ring Dean's sister made Vanessa long ago, and the journal in which Vanessa wrote the first draft of her novel about her affair with her husband's best friend. Ginny, Jill, Jackie, Celine, Valerie, and Valerie's new boyfriend stand in a circle, remembering Vanessa. The boyfriend is strong and bearded and handsome, built like a linebacker, not lean and lanky like Valerie's sea captain father. They are all happy that Valerie has a partner whom she loves and who loves her.

They reminisce about Vanessa and throw a few of her ashes into the sea. Valerie will keep the rest. They are all she has left of her mother.

As Jill drives north to Mendocino, she thinks of her mother and father; of her lost sister, Meg; of Margo and Emma and Genevieve; of Labelle and Pip and Vanessa. All gone.

This is how life is, she swallows. *You are born; you grow up; you die. You love as well as you can; you write as well as you can; you have as much sex as you can; you treat others as generously as you can; you tell the truth if you can. If you're lucky, you make new friends, and you keep the old. Some are silver, and the others, if they don't frighten you half to death, are gold.*

END

ACKNOWLEDGMENTS

Writing is a strange business. You tell a story and pray someone will want to read it, maybe even buy it.

Throughout my life, many people have inspired, nurtured and sometimes bankrolled, my writing. Here are some of them:

I'd be dead, certainly never born, without my parents, Sissy Rightor Futcher and Palmer H. Futcher, who supported my dream of becoming a writer in every way they could. One of the greatest gifts they gave me was enrolling me in a month-long summer writing seminar for high school students at Phillips Exeter Academy in New Hampshire. A dozen teens met for four hours a day, five days a week, reading and sharing our words and works, and ever so tentatively embracing the venerated title of writer.

Three beloved English professors helped fuel my desire to write by presenting the best of English literature in lively and engaging ways: Thank you, professors Mary Aswell Doll, Bettie Anne Doebler, and Helen Vendler.

Writing groups at college, graduate school, and beyond provided friendship, feedback, editorial help and emotional support when self-doubt threatened to hijack any literary project I undertook. When I moved to California from New York City in 1977 with the dream of writing a novel, authors Lee Prickett Wagner and Cleo Jones invited me to join their novel-writing group, providing invaluable editorial suggestions and encouragement for my first novel, *Crush*.

Many of the stories in *Heat* were written in the 1990s, when I joined another writing group, two of whose members, Linnea Due and Lucy Jane Bledsoe, edited anthologies that included several of the stories in *Heat*. I'm grateful to them and to the other editors and publishers who took a chance on my stories when there were very few outlets for lesbian fiction. Thank you, Mara Wild, Mikaya Heart, Karen Barber, John Keller, Judith P. Stelboum, Esther Rothblum, Jacqueline S. Weinstock, and Leslea Newman.

To writer and publisher Angela Yarber of Tehom Center, kudos for your courage, resolve, and chutzpah in bringing *Heat* and so many other unique lesbian titles to print. I'm also grateful to Tehom's Elizabeth Lee, who worked closely with me on proofing the interior galley of the manuscript.

The stories in *Heat* would not have been written without inspiration from and/or the assistance of the following people: Catherine Judith Hopkins; Anne Santos Paxson; Anne Rightor Thornton; Jean Prema; Jane Spahr; Abigail Hemstreet; David Lebe; Ter DePuy; Joan Alden; Penny Magrane; Zabelle Norwood; Margaret Kent; Ginger Morton; Ellen D. Reeder; Katherine Santos Harrison; Kate Black; Gwendolen M. Futcher; Chaparral; Elisa Odabashian; Brian Kellman; Harriet Kellman; Beverly Rich Kahn; Robert Kahn, and Mie Toyokawa.

The generosity, insight, friendship, and humor of Marny Hall and Nanette Gartrell have kept me on a more or less even keel through the last forty years. Thank you!

Finally, for her love, humor, patience, and originality, I am grateful to my wife, Erin Carney, who deserves a heaven of gold stars and a million standing ovations for supporting my writing long after she discovered how little it pays and how much time it can take from activities that often seem a whole lot more fun: traveling, hiking, hanging out with friends and family, and having sex, to name a few.

Nam Kirn and Jamila, thank you for sharing your mother with me.

Forrest and Sarib Jot, talk to me first if you are thinking of becoming a writer!